SECRET MISSIONS

STAR WARS®

THE CLONE WARS™

CURSE OF THE BLACK HOLE PIRATES

BY RYDER WINDHAM
COVER ILLUSTRATED BY WAYNE LO

Grosset & Dunlap
An Imprint of Penguin Group (USA) Inc.

LucasBooks

GROSSET & DUNLAP
Published by the Penguin Group
Penguin Group (USA) Inc., 375 Hudson Street, New York, New York 10014, USA
Penguin Group (Canada), 90 Eglinton Avenue East, Suite 700,
Toronto, Ontario M4P 2Y3, Canada
(a division of Pearson Penguin Canada Inc.)
Penguin Books Ltd., 80 Strand, London WC2R 0RL, England
Penguin Group Ireland, 25 St. Stephen's Green, Dublin 2,
Ireland (a division of Penguin Books Ltd.)
Penguin Group (Australia), 250 Camberwell Road, Camberwell, Victoria 3124,
Australia (a division of Pearson Australia Group Pty. Ltd.)
Penguin Books India Pvt. Ltd., 11 Community Centre, Panchsheel Park,
New Delhi—110 017, India
Penguin Group (NZ), 67 Apollo Drive, Rosedale, North Shore 0632,
New Zealand (a division of Pearson New Zealand Ltd.)
Penguin Books (South Africa) (Pty.) Ltd., 24 Sturdee Avenue,
Rosebank, Johannesburg 2196, South Africa

Penguin Books Ltd., Registered Offices:
80 Strand, London WC2R 0RL, England

This book is published in partnership with LucasBooks, a division of Lucasfilm Ltd.

The publisher does not have any control over and does not assume any responsibility for
author or third-party websites or their content.

Copyright © 2010 Lucasfilm Ltd. & ® or ™ where indicated. All Rights Reserved.
Used Under Authorization. Published by Grosset & Dunlap, a division of
Penguin Young Readers Group, 345 Hudson Street, New York, New York 10014.
GROSSET & DUNLAP is a trademark of Penguin Group (USA) Inc.
Printed in the U.S.A.

Library of Congress Cataloging-in-Publication Data is available.

ISBN 978-0-448-45393-4

10 9 8 7 6 5 4 3 2 1

CHAPTER 1

Cad Bane was watching a holovid and cleaning his teeth with a small, durasteel ice pick when a warning light flashed on the console in his starship's cockpit. His ship's computer announced, "Approaching Bogden system. Exiting hyperspace in three minutes."

Still picking at his teeth, Bane switched off the holovid. He had been watching *The Bounty Hunters' Guild's Greatest Hits: Volume VII*, a collected edition of holorecorded assassinations. Even though the holovid was a pirated version, it included the Guild's exclusive bonus feature of techniques for killing amphibious targets. Bane had hoped he might learn some new tricks, but he was more than halfway through the holovid, and all he'd gotten out of it was a few laughs. The two Trandoshans were especially entertaining. Cradossk was the Bounty Hunters' Guild's leader and Bossk was his son. They never agreed, and they fought constantly. Bane thought they were a riot.

Outside the cockpit, the faster-than-light dimension known as hyperspace appeared as a radiant cascade that flowed over and past Bane's ship. He swiveled his seat, turning away from the deactivated holoprojector so he could run a quick check on the propulsion and navigation systems.

At first, all systems looked fine, but then he noted a negligible fluctuation in the null quantum field generator. As good as he was at creating chaos, Bane's real skill was his ability to gather and organize data that allowed him to control circumstances. He liked everything to operate *his* way.

Bane's ship was named the *Sleight of Hand*. Although it appeared to be a battered freighter, it was actually a heavily modified Telgorn dropship. Bane had done most of the work himself. The hull was military-grade armor, and the upgraded hyperdrive could deliver him across the galaxy in a fraction of the time required by most ships. Weaponry included a top-mounted laser turret for ship-to-ship combat and pulverizing obstructive asteroids, a pair of heavy laser cannons to inflict even more lethal damage, and an ion cannon that Bane had used more than a few times to disable merchant cargo ships. A sophisticated sensor jammer rendered the *Sleight of Hand* invisible to most scanners.

Bane placed the ice pick lengthwise between his teeth, freeing his hands to push buttons on the engineering console until he corrected the fluctuation. Satisfied that the null quantum field generator now performed at a better than optimum level, he removed the ice pick from his teeth and gave the sharp tool a playful spin between his nimble, blue fingers.

He got up out of his seat and moved behind the cockpit to inspect his cargo, taking the ice pick with him. He stopped beside a two-meter-long, black plastoid box that rested on a hovering gravsled, which he'd magnetically anchored to the wall. A switch was on the box's side. Bane pressed the switch and the box's upper lid slid back, revealing a transparisteel coffin. Through the transparisteel,

Bane could clearly see the unconscious, motionless form of Jedi Master Ring-Sol Ambase.

The coffin was actually an exotic stasis pod. A life system monitor was embedded into its side, and a thin layer of ice had formed over it. With surgical precision, Bane made a quick jab with the ice pick, shattering the ice without damaging the screen. Bane leaned close to the monitor so he could read the Jedi's vital signs on a data display.

Ambase's condition had not changed. He was close to death, just as he had been ever since Bane had sealed his body in the coffin on the planet Kynachi. Whether Ambase lived or died depended entirely on how one was inclined to adjust the coffin's controls. Bane would have gladly killed the Jedi on the spot, but he hadn't been contracted to end Ambase's life, only to transport him from Kynachi to the fifth moon in the Bogden system.

Bane sealed the plastoid box, then tucked the ice pick into his gun belt as he moved back to the cockpit. Just as he returned to his seat, the hyperdrive engine began to wind down. He squinted his bulbous red eyes, and watched the bright cascade of hyperspace wash away and vanish through the cockpit window.

The *Sleight of Hand* dropped out of hyperspace without the slightest shudder. From the cockpit, Bane viewed a large planet that rested against a field of stars. He did not have to consult any data readouts to identify the planet Bogden, an unstable world with numerous moons, but he checked the navigational display anyway to confirm it was working properly. He did this out of habit, part of his ongoing routine to ensure that he would never, ever be a victim of anyone or anything, including faulty technology.

He turned his attention to a sensor scope, and focused the long-range sensors on Bogden's fifth moon, Bogg 5. The scope displayed a stream of data, including multiple layers of transmissions. Bane quickly learned that five ships were traveling to the moon and three were leaving. None of the ships were moving at excessive speed, listed as "stolen," or betrayed any awareness of the *Sleight of Hand*'s arrival in the Bogden system.

Filtering the transmissions, Bane intercepted a unique one, a signal that came from a small, artificial satellite in Bogg 5's orbit. The signal appeared as a flashing green dot on his scope, and a tiny readout indicated that the signal was broadcast on a secure frequency. The satellite was spherical, barely half a meter in diameter.

Bane knew the signal was for him, and him alone. He tuned his subspace transceiver to the signal, and tapped in a preset pass code. Had he entered the wrong code, the satellite would have exploded. Because he entered the correct code, he immediately received a set of coordinates for his next destination. The coordinates were for an unpopulated area on Bogg 5, a wide stretch of land eighty kilometers north of Mong'tar City.

Bane made a series of adjustments to his sensor controls, bounced a transmission off a triangulation of satellites over Bogg 5's far side, and zeroed in on the just-received coordinates. His sensors revealed a single starship had already landed there, and was waiting for him. The starship was a *Punworcca 116*-class interstellar sloop, a solar sailer.

Bane widened his scan beyond the edges of the Bogden system. More ships, more transmissions, many asteroids, and various radiation trails popped and flittered across his scopes. The sensors did not reveal any unusual traffic or gravitational anomalies, but Bane did not let that stop him from being extra cautious. As far as he was concerned, anyone who put all his trust in sensors was not just a fool, but a fool who got what he deserved.

He plotted his own roundabout course to Bogg 5's surface. He believed there was always a chance that someone was after him. For this reason, he had developed another special skill, which was staying ahead of everyone else. Until he was absolutely certain that he was not being monitored or followed, he wouldn't go anywhere near the solar sailer that awaited him at the designated coordinates.

Nearly two hours later, Bane circled the landing area, a broad expanse of barren black rock, and then landed the *Sleight of Hand* ten meters from the solar sailer. Exiting his ship, he stepped out onto the hard ground, looked to the solar sailer, and saw a lone, hooded figure approaching. As the figure neared, Bane saw it was a humanoid female, her face partially lost in the shadow of her cloak. She had chalk white skin and eyes so pale that had she not been walking, Bane might have assumed she was dead.

"You're late," said Asajj Ventress.

"I had to be sure I wasn't followed," Bane said, "and that you didn't bring any friends."

"Friends?" Ventress said with a sneer.

Bane grinned. "I brought something for you. Do you want it or not?"

Asajj Ventress nodded and Bane led her into the *Sleight of Hand*. He showed her the black plastoid box, and opened it to reveal the transparisteel coffin that contained Ring-Sol Ambase's motionless body. He pointed to the fresh layer of ice over the life system monitor and said, "The ice buildup is normal for this unit. Means everything's working right."

"It means your stasis pod is an antique," Ventress said disdainfully.

Ignoring her comment, Bane continued, "To view the monitor and access the controls, you just break off the ice. Like this." He removed the ice pick from his gun belt and jabbed it expertly into the ice. The ice cracked and fell free.

Ventress examined the controls, then leaned over the coffin and studied Jedi Master Ring-Sol Ambase's face. Not a trace of air escaped his nostrils. He was completely inert.

Cad Bane said, "I was told I'd be getting more instructions."

Rising away from the coffin, Ventress turned

to face Bane. "You're going to Bilbringii. But first, move the pod to my ship," she said. "I'll take the ice pick, too."

"Get your own ice pick," Bane said as he returned the tool to his belt. "This one's mine."

After the stasis pod was transferred to the solar sailer, Ventress watched the bounty hunter's ship rise away from Bogg 5's surface. When the ship had vanished into the sky, she took a seat beside the droid pilot in the solar sailer's bubble cockpit and instructed the droid to lift off.

Ventress went to the main hold to inspect her cargo. The stasis pod that contained Ambase rested beside a second stasis pod that was contemporary in design. On top of the second pod was a Republic Army-issued white helmet with a T-visor, which until recently had been worn by the pod's unconscious occupant. Ventress confirmed both pods were operating efficiently before returning to the cockpit.

The solar sailer flew directly to another Bogden moon, the ancient tombworld named Kohlma.

Shortly after the sleek vessel began its descent through Kohlma's atmosphere, it passed through gray clouds and angled toward a high mountain. The mountain was topped by a dark castle with a central dome, surrounded by spined spires that appeared to be growing up from their rocky perch. Rain pelted the solar sailer as it landed on a pad that jutted out from the base of the castle's dome.

The solar sailer's landing ramp extended and Ventress walked down it. She pulled back her cowl and turned her ghastly face up to the sky, squeezing her eyes shut as the rain spattered against her head.

"You're late," said a deep voice from the castle's nearby entrance.

Ventress opened her eyes as she turned to face the tall, well-groomed, immaculately attired man who stood in the vaulted doorway. He was Count Dooku, the former Jedi Master who was now the leader of the Separatist Alliance.

"Blame the bounty hunter," Ventress said. "He was late first."

Dooku lifted one eyebrow. "I trust he remains unaware of your own mission to Kynachi?"

Ventress nodded. "I obtained a . . . companion

for Ambase. As you wished."

Dooku stepped away from the doorway, his dark cape flowing behind him. A disc-shaped repulsorlift device hovered in the air above his head. The device moved along with him, projecting a thin energy shield around his body to deflect the rain and keep him dry as he approached Ventress. He gestured to the nearby light freighter and said, "Prepare that ship for a crash landing."

"A crash landing? But why?"

"Do as I say," Dooku commanded.

Ventress stared hard at her Master for a moment, then slunk away from him, heading for the light freighter.

Dooku left his rain-repelling device hovering above the landing ramp as he entered the solar sailer. Inside the main hold, he found the two stasis pods. Ignoring the newer pod and the white helmet that rested on it, he stepped beside the black plastoid box and slid back its lid. He gazed at the unconscious Jedi Master who lay in the transparisteel coffin.

Brushing his fingers across the coffin's freezing surface, Dooku smiled and said, "It's been a long time, old friend."

CHAPTER 2

Nuru Kungurama had a lot on his mind.

By an incredible series of circumstances, the Padawan was on a smuggler's freighter, traveling across the galaxy with a squad of four Republic clone troopers and a reprogrammed droid commando. They were on a secret mission, heading for a space station in orbit of Nuru's distant homeworld, the planet Csilla, in Chiss space. This was especially incredible because Nuru was only a Jedi apprentice, and his assignment had come from Supreme Chancellor Palpatine himself.

Events are moving too fast.

Chiss space was in the Unknown Regions, far

beyond the galaxy's Outer Rim. Even though Nuru and his allies were traveling at faster-than-light speed through hyperspace, their destination was so remote that the journey required several layovers and detours through real space, and nearly ten days. If Nuru had ever been to Chiss space before, he had no memory of it.

Except for my own reflection, I've never even seen another Chiss.

Since infancy, he had been raised at the Jedi Temple on Coruscant. Although Coruscant was home to countless alien immigrants, some of whom had blue skin and red eyes, Chiss had been among the planet's greatest minorities. As for Jedi Archives, it had more information about the rare energy spiders of Kessel than it had for all of Chiss space.

I've never been so far from the Temple.

Just a few days earlier, on Coruscant, Jedi Master Ring-Sol Ambase had been preparing to leave on a mission when Nuru had a premonition that Ambase would not return. Nuru's previous Master, Lanchu Skaa, had died at the Battle of Geonosis, the historic conflict that launched the civil war between the Galactic Republic and the Separatist Alliance. Nuru still felt the immense loss of Master Skaa, and it pained him that Skaa had left him on Coruscant without saying good-bye. He knew it was not Skaa's fault. Nuru believed Skaa would have said good-bye if he had had the opportunity, as well as the foresight that he would never see his apprentice again.

Will I ever return to Coruscant?

Determined not to lose his second Master, Nuru had stealthily boarded the ship that would transport Ambase and three squads of clone troopers to the planet Kynachi. He had only wanted to help.

The mission was a disaster. The Techno Union's Separatist forces, led by the Skakoan Overseer Umbrag, ambushed the Republic ship in orbit of Kynachi. The ship's escape pods had been sabotaged. Several clone troopers died. And Ambase vanished.

Did one of the troopers sabotage the escape pods? Or was it someone else?

Fortunately, Nuru and a group of clone troopers survived. They found new allies, including the pilot Lalo Gunn, captain of the *Hasty Harpy*, and the droid commando that they refurbished and named Cleaver. Working together, they rescued captive clone troopers from a Kynachi prison and liberated

Kynachi from the Techno Union. They became the Breakout Squad.

I was never trained to command a squad of troopers.

Despite the victory over the Techno Union, Nuru had expected to be expelled from the Jedi Order because he had left Coruscant without permission. Instead, Supreme Chancellor Palpatine convinced Master Yoda to allow the troopers of the Breakout Squad to escort Nuru to Csilla for a diplomatic assignment in Chiss space.

The Chancellor himself had provided the instructions for Nuru, along with navigational coordinates for the series of hyperspace jumps that were required to reach the Chiss homeworld. The Chancellor had also transmitted a small amount of data about Chiss culture, including a concise interactive guide to the Chiss language, Cheunh, and an allegedly easier trade language, Minnisiat. Nuru could barely comprehend either language.

We should have brought a protocol droid.

Nuru took some consolation in that the Chancellor's instructions were extremely brief. He was to meet a Chiss named Sev'eere'nuruodo at a space station, and find out if the Chiss had a specific interest in opening diplomatic relations with the Galactic Republic.

Could it be a trap?

Nuru couldn't imagine that the Chancellor would knowingly send him into a dangerous situation. But as he considered the possibility, he realized he'd moved his hand to brush his fingers against the two lightsabers that were clipped to his belt. He had built one of the lightsabers himself, and received the second from a mysterious Duros bounty hunter, who claimed he had found it on Kynachi. The second lightsaber had been Master Ambase's weapon.

My Master is alive. I know he is!

The last time Nuru had seen his silver-haired Master was on a small viewscreen, a moment before Ambase's escape pod jettisoned from the doomed freighter to Kynachi. Nuru wondered if Ambase had been abducted by Overseer Umbrag, who'd fled Kynachi in his Metalorn yacht before the arrival of Republic reinforcements.

Even though Nuru was not by himself as he traveled through hyperspace, he felt terribly alone.

I have to clear my mind.

He took a deep breath and began to meditate. He was still meditating almost an hour later, when he became aware of loud noises behind him. He knew who was responsible.

The Breakout Squad.

Lalo Gunn was seated in the cockpit of her freighter, the *Hasty Harpy*, when she heard a loud crash from behind in the main cabin. The *Harpy* was hurtling through hyperspace, and Gunn was afraid that the noise was a malfunction in the hyperdrive engine. A moment later, she heard a second crash, louder than the first. She glanced at a diagnostic display, searching for any sign of technical failure or damage.

Then came two more crashes in quick succession, followed by a rapid hammering noise.

Gunn grabbed a hydrospanner that dangled from a hook on the side of her seat as she scrambled out of the cockpit. Ducking through a short passage tube, she held the hydrospanner out like a weapon as she moved fast into the main cabin, but what she found there made her come to an abrupt stop.

One fully-armored clone trooper was engaged in a fight with a droid commando. Both opponents were using long durasteel rods to strike each other, producing loud clashing noises.

Two more troopers were prone on the deck, side by side, doing incredibly fast push-ups. As they bent their elbows and lowered their armored torsos, their chins touched the cabin's metal deck.

A fourth trooper was partially stretched out upon an acceleration couch with his fingers interlocked behind his head. Wearing a black body glove, he had both legs braced under a neighboring worktable, which gave him traction while he performed vigorous sit-ups.

Then Gunn noticed the young, blue-skinned Jedi. He was easy to miss because he was the only one in the room who wasn't moving a muscle, and his dark tunic helped him blend in with the cabin's drab interior. The boy stood by himself, head slightly lowered, hands clasped behind his back as he faced the cabin's far corner, apparently oblivious to the troopers. Gunn shouted, "What in blazes is going on back here?!"

All four troopers and the droid commando froze, then turned their necks to look at Gunn. For a moment, the only sound in the cabin was the steady hum of the hyperdrive engine. The young Jedi did not flinch and kept his back to everyone.

Gunn shifted her angered gaze at the trooper who'd been doing sit-ups. The trooper held Gunn's gaze and replied, "Sorry, Captain Gunn. We're just exercising."

Still holding the hydrospanner, Gunn made a sweeping gesture with her arm and added, "Does my main cabin look like a gymnasium?!"

"I'm sorry, too, Captain," said the trooper who'd been sparring with the droid commando. He pulled off his helmet, revealing swarthy features that were identical to the other troopers. Gesturing to the droid commando beside him, he continued, "Cleaver and I didn't mean to be so loud. Right, Cleaver?"

The droid named Cleaver nodded. "That is correct," Cleaver said through the grilled vocabulator at the base of his head. "Our only intention was to strike each other with blunt instruments." Although he appeared to be a standard-model Separatist droid commando, Cleaver was actually a refurbished unit, built from scavenged parts, including logic and behavioral circuits salvaged from the brain of Gunn's ruined navigation droid, Teejay.

The two other troopers got up from the deck where they'd been doing push-ups. "Please accept our apologies, Captain. If the boys and I don't keep up our physical training, we can get a bit restless."

"Oh, knock it off with the apologies already," Gunn said. "If it weren't for you guys, I'd still be stuck on Kynachi. But when I agreed to haul you off that rock, I didn't know I was signing on for such a long haul! We're going to be stuck in this crate for over a week, but time will pass a lot faster if you learn to relax a little." Then she looked at the one clone who hadn't spoken and she added, "As for you, Chatterbox, I'm just disappointed. You could've been sitting in the cockpit with me, enjoying the view of hyperspace, but instead, you're back here doing push-ups with your pals. Honestly!"

Chatterbox was baffled by Gunn's remark. He glanced at his three allies and saw they all wore similarly confused expressions.

Before any of the troopers could respond, Gunn continued, "Why is the Jedi facing the corner? Are you guys punishing him or something?"

Without turning to face Gunn or the others, Nuru replied, "I'm meditating."

Gunn laughed. "Meditating, huh? Kid, if you could tune out the racket these guys were making, you must be very good at it."

Breaker, the trooper who'd been sparring with Cleaver, said, "He's been standing there like that for over an hour."

Looking away from Nuru, Gunn returned her attention to the troopers. "We'll be dropping out of hyperspace in about fifteen minutes," she said. "It'll be just a short layover in the Fakir sector, but everyone should be belted into their seats when we exit." Then she looked directly at Chatterbox and added, "The hyperspace routes that the Chancellor provided for the next two jumps are kind of tricky. In case you didn't notice, my ship is minus one navigator droid, so I'll need another set of eyes to monitor the navi-computer."

The trooper who'd been doing sit-ups said, "I'd be happy to help, too, Captain. My eyes are good. Our former commander named me Sharp because he thought I had sharp eyesight."

Keeping her gaze on Chatterbox, Gunn replied, "That's a nice story, Sharp, but I ain't talkin' to you." Then she winked at Chatterbox and added, "See you in the cockpit." She turned and stepped out of the cabin, heading back through the passage tube.

Chatterbox once again surveyed the expressions of the other clones. Sharp said, "Did I miss something earlier?"

"Yeah, you did," said Knuckles, the trooper who had been competing with Chatterbox to see who could do the most push-ups. "On Kynachi, before we rescued you, when Commander Nuru introduced Chatterbox to Gunn, Gunn mentioned that she liked men who keep their mouths shut."

Sharp said, "Really?" He looked straight at the silent trooper and said, "Chatterbox, are you deliberately keeping your mouth shut so Gunn will like you?"

Chatterbox shook his head.

"Well," Sharp said, "clearly, it's not Chatterbox's fault."

"Yeah, clearly," said Knuckles. "I thought Gunn was just joking about how much she liked Chatterbox, but I sort of get the impression she *means* it."

Breaker sighed. "They didn't teach us how to deal with situations like *this* back on Kamino."

Sharp stroked his chin thoughtfully, then said, "I think I know why Gunn *really* likes Chatterbox."

Breaker, Knuckles, and Chatterbox all turned to face Sharp. Speaking at the same time, Breaker and Knuckles said, "Why?"

"Isn't it obvious?" Sharp said. "It's because he's so much better-looking than the rest of us."

The clones looked at one another, and then Breaker, Knuckles, and Sharp burst out laughing. Chatterbox just rolled his eyes. The three troopers were still laughing when Cleaver said unexpectedly, "What is *meditating*?"

The troopers looked at Cleaver, who had turned his white photoreceptors to gaze at Nuru's back. Before any of the troopers could offer an answer to Cleaver, Nuru replied, "To meditate is to relax the mind as well as the body. To relax my mind, I think of nothing."

Cleaver said, "This helps you fight your enemies?"

"Yes," Nuru said. "And also helps my allies."

Cleaver shook his head. "I do not understand,"

he said. "When you look away from all others, and you are not holding a weapon, are you not more vulnerable to an attack?"

"Commander Nuru has special abilities, Cleaver," Breaker interjected. "He's a Jedi. He draws his power from some mystical energy called the Force."

"The Force?" Cleaver said. He shook his head again. "I've never heard of that before. I have so much to learn."

Breaker said, "Begging your pardon, Commander Nuru, but I wonder if Cleaver has a point. That is, about you being vulnerable while meditating. For example, how could you stop an assassin from shooting you in the back?"

Nuru answered calmly, "If you were an assassin, how fast could you fire your blaster?"

Cleaver and the other troopers looked at Breaker, waiting for his response. Breaker kept his own eyes fixed on the back of Nuru's head as he said, "Begging your pardon again, Commander Nuru, but . . . well, even with the Force, I don't see how you'd stand a chance."

Nuru said, "I suppose there's only one way

to find out. I'll continue standing here, facing the corner, while you set your blaster pistol to stun. For safety's sake, I suggest you put your helmet back on. Then you may fire whenever you're ready."

Looking from Nuru to Breaker, Cleaver said, "Commander Nuru, may I ask how you knew that Master Breaker had removed his helmet if you did not *see* him do it?"

"Because when he wears his helmet, he speaks through a comlink microphone," Nuru answered. "One can hear the difference."

"Oh," Cleaver said. "I must listen more carefully."

Ignoring the droid, Breaker said, "Commander Nuru, you're not serious, are you? I mean, about me shooting at you?"

"I'm quite serious," Nuru said. "Consider this a test. If do you strike me, I'll only be knocked out briefly. If you don't, we'll all learn a different lesson. Go on, Breaker. Reset your blaster, then draw it and fire. Give it your best shot."

Breaker looked at the other troopers. Sharp said, "I don't think this is a good idea."

Knuckles said, "I don't, either, but . . . if we're to

learn a lesson, I'd rather learn it here and now than under less controlled circumstances."

More confused than ever, Cleaver said, "Does meditating usually lead to people firing blasters inside starships?"

"Maybe just this one time, Cleaver," Nuru said. "Breaker, I'm ready when you are."

"All right, Commander," Breaker said. "But I sincerely hope you know what you're doing." He put his helmet back on, then said, "I'm reaching to my pistol now, but only to reset it." He moved his right hand to the holster secured against the armor that covered his right hip. After using his black-gloved thumb to set the blaster on stun, he shifted his hand away from the holster. The other troopers and Cleaver moved away from Breaker, giving him room.

Breaker gazed through his helmet's T-visor, keeping his eyes fixed on the back of Nuru's tunic, at the area between the boy's shoulder blades. Nuru's hands remained gently clasped behind his back. Breaker did not have to look at the optical readout in his visor to estimate the distance between him and the young Jedi. He could clearly see it was barely three meters.

Breaker's right hand wavered beside his holster, and then his arm went slack. He sighed. "I don't think I can do this, Commander Nuru," he said. "Shooting a Jedi goes completely against all my training on Kamino."

"You're still assuming you'll hit me, Breaker," Nuru said. "Remember, this is only a test. A stun won't kill me. Trust me."

"I do trust you," Breaker said, "but I *can't* do this. It just feels . . . wrong."

"What if I gave you a direct order?"

Breaker shook his head and said, "I don't know."

"Then I order you to draw your weapon and shoot me."

Breaker moved fast, and without hesitation. The fingers of his right hand were still racing toward his blaster's grip when Nuru—having already sensed the movement from behind—sent his own hand flying to his belt. Nuru seized his lightsaber, leaving his Master's weapon dangling from its clip.

The blaster leaped into Breaker's hand. At the same moment, Nuru activated his lightsaber, igniting its blue blade of pure energy as he spun to face Breaker.

Breaker's arm swung up and he squeezed the blaster's trigger, launching a fiery laser bolt at Nuru's chest. Nuru kept his red eyes locked on Breaker's T-visor as he shifted his wrists slightly, rapidly adjusting the angle of his lightsaber to meet the oncoming bolt.

The bolt struck the blade and bounced back at Breaker, smacking into the armor plate that covered his upper left arm. Although the stunning bolt carried a diminished charge, the impact made Breaker flinch and his left leg buckled under him. He squeezed off another shot before he went down on his left knee.

Nuru's blade flicked through the air again, smacking the second bolt into the metal deck as he leaped forward. Holding tight to his lightsaber with one hand, he lashed out with the other and plucked the pistol out of Breaker's hand. Breaker's response was pure reflex as his own hand launched after the pistol and clamped around Nuru's wrist.

Breaker gasped, "You . . . you're all right, Commander Nuru?"

"I'm fine, Breaker," Nuru said, his voice eerily unemotional as he deactivated his lightsaber. "If this had been a real assassination attempt, I wouldn't have just taken your weapon away. You can let go of my wrist now."

Only then did Breaker realize that he was still gripping Nuru's wrist. As Breaker released his hold, Sharp stepped over beside Knuckles and Chatterbox and muttered, "I had no idea Commander Nuru could move so fast!"

Cleaver said, "Perhaps *I* should try meditating?"

Gunn came running back into the main cabin. She bellowed, "Don't tell me that wasn't blaster fire I just heard!" Then she noticed the helmeted trooper kneeling in front of Nuru. She also saw that Nuru held the trooper's blaster pistol in one hand and his lightsaber in the other.

Gunn shook her head with disgust. "I'm not even going to *ask* what you two were up to," she said. "I want you all to grab a seat and get belted in now! Everyone but *you*, that is." She stepped over to the three standing troopers and grabbed one by the arm. "Let's go, Chatterbox," she said. "You're coming to the cockpit right now!" She hauled the astonished trooper toward the passage tube.

As soon as Gunn and the trooper had exited the

cabin, Cleaver said, "Unless my short-term memory is faulty, I believe Captain Gunn has mistaken Sharp for Chatterbox."

Knuckles said, "Cleaver, you took the words right out of my mouth."

He looked to Chatterbox, who was in fact still standing beside him. Knuckles said, "Chatterbox, maybe you should have said something before Gunn dragged Sharp off with her?"

Chatterbox shrugged.

Breaker was still kneeling on the deck beside Nuru. As Nuru handed the blaster pistol back to him, Breaker said, "I'm sorry."

"You've no reason to be," Nuru said as he clipped his lightsaber to his belt. "I owe *you* an apology. I didn't mean to make you fall on your injured leg. Here, let me help you up."

"Thanks," Breaker said as he placed a hand on the boy's shoulder. Rising to his feet, he said, "I'm glad to know you can defend yourself, Commander Nuru, but . . . I hope you never give me an order like that again!" He removed his helmet, then reached up to rub the side of his head. "Going against my basic training makes my brain ache."

Just then, Gunn's angry shouts echoed down from the cockpit.

"Uh-oh," Knuckles said. "Sounds like Captain Gunn just sorted out that she's not with Chatterbox."

A few seconds later, Sharp returned to the main cabin. Facing Chatterbox, he said, "I *tried* identifying myself to Captain Gunn before we reached the cockpit." He aimed a thumb at the passage tube and added, "She'd like to have a word with you."

Chatterbox's brow furrowed. He turned to face Nuru. Nuru said, "It might be best if you go and listen to what she has to say, Chatterbox. Keep in mind, she *is* the captain of this vessel."

Chatterbox sighed.

As he stepped into the passage tube to the cockpit, he muttered, "Duty calls."

Nuru gestured to the cabin's seats. "We'd best buckle up. We'll be exiting hyperspace soon."

Knuckles, Sharp, and Breaker seated themselves on the acceleration couch, a padded bench with a mismatched conform-lounge back. Cleaver looked at the two remaining seats, then said, "Commander Nuru, does one have to stand in order to meditate, or can it be done while sitting?"

"Either way," Nuru said. "Why do you ask?"

Cleaver gestured to the nearest empty seat and said, "With your permission, Commander, may I sit there so I can face the corner? I would like to try meditating."

Nuru did not know whether any droid was capable of meditating, but he said politely, "Of course, Cleaver. The corner is yours."

As he arranged himself in his seat, Cleaver glanced back at Nuru and said, "I have never thought of nothing before."

Nuru smiled. "Take your time."

CHAPTER 3

"I do not believe I am meditating correctly, Commander Nuru," Cleaver said from his seat in the *Hasty Harpy*'s main cabin.

The droid had been silent for days, and his voice surprised Nuru. Nuru was sitting beside Breaker on the other side of the cabin, viewing a holographic star chart. The *Harpy* was once again traveling through hyperspace, on the last leg of her journey into the Unknown Regions.

Cleaver continued, "I have been staring at this corner for one hundred and forty-six hours, eleven minutes, and thirty-eight seconds and counting, but my behavioral circuitry matrix is the same as before

I started. How will I know when I am relaxed?"

"I'm not sure I'm qualified to answer that question, Cleaver," Nuru said, ignoring Knuckles and Sharp as they arm-wrestled on the cabin's workbench. "To be honest," Nuru continued, "I have no idea whether droids *can* meditate."

Cleaver said, "Oh."

Hearing the disappointment in the droid's voice, Nuru added, "But you certainly *looked* like you were meditating, Cleaver. You didn't even budge when Breaker transmitted the Chancellor's Chiss linguistic data onto your language memory disc."

"He did?" Cleaver said, surprised. "I did not know I even had a language memory disc."

"For what it's worth," Nuru added, "I don't know of any Jedi who ever sat still for so long."

Rising from his seat, Cleaver flexed his metal arms and said, "I believe my joints do feel a bit more relaxed. Perhaps I did use my time wisely."

"Ha!" Knuckles said as he slammed Sharp's arm down against the workbench. "That's 517 to 483! Wait'll I tell Chatterbox!"

"You'll have to wait for Captain Gunn to release him from navi-computer monitoring duty," Sharp said as he unlocked his fingers from Knuckles' grasp. "Maybe we should try wrestling with our left arms for a change?"

Without looking away from the star chart, Breaker said, "Actually, you two might want to postpone the next match. If the charts and data provided by the Chancellor's office are correct, we'll be arriving in orbit of Csilla in fifty-two minutes."

Thanks to their respective training and conditioning, Nuru and the troopers were physically and psychologically prepared for long journeys in relatively confined spaces. Still, after so many days in the *Hasty Harpy*, all the time sleeping in rotation because the freighter's crew quarters only had three bunks, they were all eager to get out.

Nuru returned his attention to the star chart to reexamine their path across and beyond the edge of the galaxy. After leaving Kynachi, they had made their way to the Entralla Route and traveled down to Ord Mantell, where they had refueled and picked up supplies. They had proceeded via the Celanon Spur past Vicondor, and down the Namadii Corridor to Dorin, homeworld of the Kel Dor. Up until that point, Lalo Gunn had been familiar with the hyperlanes, but she was not daunted by the loss of her navigator droid, Teejay. In fact, she seemed most enthusiastic about training Chatterbox to help her operate her freighter.

Using the navigational coordinates provided by Chancellor Palpatine, they had arrived in the Mondress Sector, and then proceeded to the Albanin Sector before they'd entered the Unknown Regions. With six more days of travel still ahead, they trusted that the Chancellor's coordinates would deliver them to Chiss space.

Turning to Nuru, Breaker said, "I imagine you're excited about seeing Csilla?"

Nuru did not answer, but stared hard at the holographic display of stars.

Breaker said, "Something wrong?"

Nuru blinked his red eyes, glanced at Breaker, then returned his gaze to the holographic display. He said, "I regret my training at the Jedi Temple didn't quite prepare me for this mission."

Knuckles and Sharp overheard Nuru's remark. "What?!" Knuckles responded. "*You*, Commander Nuru? Not prepared? How can you say that after the way you handled yourself on Kynachi?"

Sharp added, "Or after the way you helped liberate Kynachi from those infernal droids?" Glancing at the droid commando on the other side of the cabin, Sharp added, "No offense, Cleaver."

"None taken, sir," Cleaver replied.

Breaker said, "Knuckles and Sharp are right, Commander Nuru. Your training at the Jedi Temple probably prepared you for more than you realize."

"Being able to fight is one thing," Nuru said. "But going on a diplomatic mission to Csilla? That's another thing entirely."

Breaker said, "Chancellor Palpatine and General Yoda wouldn't have sent you to Csilla if they didn't believe you were ready."

Nuru shook his head. "You don't understand, Breaker," he said. "I've never met another Chiss. Ever. I don't like to admit this but . . . well, I'm nervous."

Sharp said, "Because you still can't understand their languages?"

"Thanks for reminding me," Nuru said. "I'm supposed to meet a diplomat whose name I can barely pronounce." He tried saying the name slowly. "*Sev'eere'nuruodo.*"

Breaker said, "You can't be nervous, Commander. Cleaver should be able to translate for you."

Surprised, Cleaver said, "I should?"

Breaker faced the droid and said, "Weren't you listening? Your language memory disc now contains Chiss linguistic data, so you can be Nuru's translator. Go on, let's hear you say something in Cheunh, like . . . 'Thank you for your hospitality.'"

A flurry of alien words came out of Cleaver's vocabulator. When he was done, Cleaver looked at Nuru and said, "I could not ascertain a Cheunh word for *hospitality*, but I incorporated synonyms for *comradely service*. Do you think that is a sufficient translation?"

"I have absolutely no idea," Nuru said, hanging his head. "But it's not the language I'm nervous about. It's . . . well, I don't know how I'll react when I see other Chiss for the first time. On Coruscant, I'm afraid I grew comfortable with the idea that I was somewhat unique, that I might never meet another Chiss. It's hard for me to imagine being among people who look like me."

"Oh, if only the boys and I had *that* problem," Knuckles said with a chuckle as he made a gesturing wave to Sharp and Breaker.

"Sorry," Nuru said. "You must think I'm being ridiculous."

"Not at all, Commander." Knuckles shook his head. "But I don't think you should be nervous that you've yet to meet another Chiss."

"Really?" Nuru said. "Why not?"

Knuckles aimed a finger at Nuru and said, "Because you're Nuru Kungurama. A Jedi. And no one in Chiss space has ever met *you* before."

Sharp said, "Nicely put, Knuckles."

Breaker clapped Nuru on the shoulder and said, "You have nothing to worry about. Everything will go fine."

"Where's Csilla?" Nuru said.

He was sitting on the small seat that folded out from the wall behind Lalo Gunn and Chatterbox in the *Hasty Harpy*'s cockpit. The *Harpy* had just dropped out of hyperspace, and the Corellian YT-1760 transport's centrally configured cockpit offered a wide field of vision. Based on the coordinates that Supreme Chancellor Palpatine had provided, Nuru had expected to arrive in sight of the planet Csilla, a large, glacial world. But as he peered past the shoulders of Gunn and Chatterbox and gazed through the cockpit's transparisteel windows, he saw only a field of distant stars.

"No nearby planets on the scopes," Gunn said. "And the nearest star is three light years away. Chatterbox, you triple-checked the navi-computer before the last jump, right?"

Chatterbox nodded.

Nuru said, "What's going on?"

Gunn said, "Our position is correct, except . . . no Csilla."

"What do you mean no Csilla?" Nuru said. "Where is it?"

"That's what I'm trying to tell you, kid. It ain't there. It's—"

"Look!" Nuru interrupted. He extended his arm past Chatterbox and pointed to the viewport. "Something's out there!"

Gunn and Chatterbox followed Nuru's gaze to see a dark, triangular object, a silhouette suspended against the starfield. Gunn consulted her sensor scopes and said, "It might be a ship or a station, but I can't tell. My sensors aren't picking up any signals." She adjusted the sensor controls and added, "Maybe it's using a sensor jammer. The scopes can't even determine that thing's size or how far away it is."

A warning light flashed on the *Harpy*'s control console. Gunn said, "We're being scanned."

In the indistinct distance across space, the dark object shifted slightly, and one of its sides seemed to swell outward. A moment later, lights flickered on across the object, revealing it had a curved surface, and that its true shape was not a triangle but a cone. The cone rotated and came to a stop so that it appeared to be inverted, with its sharply tapered end pointing "down" from the *Harpy*'s perspective.

Another light flashed on the *Harpy*'s console. From the comlink, a strangely neutral but synthetic voice said, "Chiss Expansionary Defense Force Station Ifpe'a to unidentified starship. State your purpose."

Gunn glanced back at Nuru. "I am Nuru Kungurama of the Jedi Order," he said. "Supreme Chancellor Palpatine of the Galactic Republic sent me here in response to a request from an ambassador of the Chiss Ascendancy, Aristocra Sev'eere'nuruodo."

After a brief silence, the synthetic voice replied, "Shut down sublight engines and all weapons systems. Await docking procedure."

Gunn muttered, "Not exactly a warm welcome."

The clone said, "I have a bad feeling about this."

"Who asked *you*?!" Gunn said as she threw a quick jab at Chatterbox's shoulder.

Nuru said, "I'm surprised that the voice from the station spoke Basic. From the data I examined, I thought the Chiss were so isolated that they're not conversant in any languages from Republic space."

"Thanks for the history lesson," Gunn said sarcastically. "So, what do we do now?"

Nuru thought hard. He was disturbed that their exit from hyperspace hadn't delivered them to Csilla. Finally, he said, "Follow their instructions. Shut down the engines and weapons. And let's keep in mind that we're invited guests, even if we didn't arrive where we expected."

"You're the boss," Gunn said.

While Gunn and Chatterbox pushed buttons and adjusted controls, Nuru kept his eyes on the conical vessel. The *Harpy*'s engines powered down, and the freighter began to drift. A moment later, the *Harpy* lurched forward, heading toward the Chiss station.

Nuru said, "Tractor beam?"

"Yup," Gunn replied, scowling.

As the invisible tractor beam drew the *Harpy* closer to the Chiss station, Nuru, Gunn, and Chatterbox realized the station was much larger than it had appeared from a distance. Gunn glanced at her scopes again and said, "Scanners are still coming up empty, but by my eye, that station's about a thousand meters tall."

A wide, triangular door slid back on the station's side, and the *Harpy* slowly glided in through the open door and into a docking bay. Dimly illuminated by yellowish lights, the docking bay consisted of an oval landing pad enveloped by a curved, pale green wall that was smooth and without windows. As the tractor beam deposited the *Harpy* on the landing pad, the bay's triangular door slid shut, sealing the bay.

The *Harpy*'s sensor scopes crackled with activity, surprising Gunn and Chatterbox. "Whoa," Gunn said. "We're picking up lots of strange energy readings." Looking at a data stream, she added, "I can't make heads or tails out of most of this info, but it looks like this bay has a breathable atmosphere."

"Let's tell the others," Nuru said as he scrambled out of the cockpit.

The *Harpy*'s landing ramp extended to the docking bay floor. Nuru was the first to emerge, followed by Cleaver, the four troopers, and Gunn. The troopers were fully armored and carried their blaster rifles slung over their shoulders.

Gunn lingered at the bottom of the landing ramp, looked around and said, "No one to greet us? Did the Chancellor's data about the Chiss say anything about a chilly reception?"

"Patience," the young Jedi said as he eyed the docking bay's smooth walls. "They are probably still scanning us."

A thin, diagonal strip of orange light pulsed against a lower section of the wall, where the wall sloped in to meet the floor. The strip of light grew brighter and expanded to reveal an illuminated doorway. A humanoid silhouette stood in the doorway, and then the mysterious figure stepped forward into the hangar.

For the first time in his life, Nuru faced another

Chiss. Like Nuru, the unidentified Chiss had blue skin, glowing red eyes, and gleaming black hair. The Chiss was attired in a crisp, black uniform with orange tabs at the collar.

Nuru had assumed that his first encounter would be with a group of Chiss, not an individual. Despite his training at the Jedi Temple, where he had learned much about staying objective and not making judgments based on immediate impressions, his very first thought as he looked at the Chiss before him was, *She's beautiful.*

CHAPTER 4

The female Chiss moved away from the illuminated doorway and came to a stop in front of Nuru. She was slightly taller than the young Jedi, but she kept her chin elevated as she faced him.

Nuru stared into the girl's red eyes. Her skin was smooth and unlined, and he suspected she was not much older than he. Her facial expression was so neutral that it held no trace of emotion. Nuru felt tongue-tied. He struggled to remember the greeting he had practiced in the Cheunh language. Unable to recall the words, he bowed at the waist.

The girl responded by widening her eyes as she took a cautious step backward.

Nuru had intended his bow as a gesture of courtesy, but realized that bowing might be inappropriate in Chiss space. Fearing that he'd either frightened or insulted the girl, he remembered the phrase he had rehearsed.

"Pavl'cha sertketch Jedi lommeeth'ree," he said, trying not to bite his tongue. "Nuru Kungurama agad nac'shu Republic depostchu'ukak tah Palpatine. Pavl'cha ferch'sti'onmell Aristocra Sev'eere'nuruodo."

The girl replied, "You are called . . . Nuru Kungurama?"

Nuru was surprised to hear the girl speak in accentless Basic. He smiled and said yes. The girl held his gaze but did not reply. Nuru continued, "I . . . I am to meet with Aristocra Sev'eere'nuruodo."

"I am Aristocra Sev'eere'nuruodo."

"Oh," Nuru said, and realized from how she'd pronounced her own name that he had pronounced it incorrectly. "I . . ." He almost blurted out, *I was expecting someone older*, but he caught himself and said instead, "I, um, didn't know you spoke Basic. And I hope you aren't upset . . . I mean, I hope you will forgive me for mispronouncing your name.

I'm afraid I . . . I'm having a difficult time learning Cheunh."

Gunn remained standing beside the *Harpy*'s landing ramp. She and Chatterbox glanced at each other, but quickly returned their attention to Nuru and the Chiss girl.

Keeping her eyes fixed on Nuru, the girl said, "You are encouraged to refer to me as Veeren. It is, you might say, an abbreviation of Sev'eere'nuruodo."

"Thank you, Veeren," Nuru said. "And you may call me Nuru."

The girl winced slightly. "I shall . . . consider it," she said.

Nuru wondered if he had offended the girl somehow. Trying hard to collect his thoughts, he remembered his mission and said, "Veeren, there is something that puzzles me. My government's leader, Supreme Chancellor Palpatine, gave us navigational coordinates that he said would deliver us to the Csilla system. However, the nearest star is light years away from our present position."

"Your leader misled you," Veeren said.

"What?" Nuru replied. "But . . . why would he do that?"

"I did not say he misled you *deliberately*," Veeren said coolly. "I merely said that he misled you. My original communication to him was quite clear, that I wished to meet with a representative of the Republic. I provided data to lead a Republic ship through hyperspace to this station. If your Chancellor inferred that the navigational coordinates would lead to Csilla, he was mistaken."

Using his Force powers, Nuru sensed that Veeren was not attempting to deceive him. Although he found her voice and manner somewhat off-putting, the way she spoke without a trace of warmth, he also sensed she wasn't hostile.

Veeren gestured to the right of the illuminated doorway. The curved wall slid silently to the side, exposing a transparent window that offered a view into an adjoining, undecorated chamber. At the center of the chamber were two large, inverted cones that echoed the shape of the space station. Hovering a few centimeters above the bare floor, the cones rotated slightly to reveal each was partially hollow and held a round seat. Nuru realized they were chairs.

Veeren said, "You and I shall adjourn to the conference room. Your companions will remain here.

They will not be able to hear us, but can monitor us through the window."

Nuru glanced back at Gunn and the troopers, then said, "But . . . well, I'm eager to talk with you, but it's been a very long journey. Is it possible that my friends might have some refreshments?"

Veeren's expression remained inscrutable as she said, "*Refreshments*?"

"Yes," Nuru said. "Food and drink?"

Veeren hesitated for a moment, then said, "Do I understand correctly, that you traveled here without food and drink? Or do you expect *me* to provide food and drink?"

"Uh, maybe not you personally," Nuru said. "Forgive me, Veeren. I am ignorant of Chiss etiquette. I meant no insult."

"No matter," Veeren said. "Our meeting will not be long," She turned for the illuminated doorway.

Nuru realized that Veeren seemed to have no interest in whether he and his allies had sufficient nourishment. Unsure whether Veeren was being deliberately rude or behaving like a typical Chiss, the young Jedi was about to follow her into the adjoining room when someone behind him said, "Ahem." It was Breaker, clearing his throat.

Both Veeren and Nuru stopped and turned to face the helmeted trooper. Nuru said, "Yes, Breaker?"

"Begging your pardon, Commander," Breaker said, "but Cleaver should accompany you. He *is* your translator, and would be most useful in the event of any accidental miscommunication between you and the aristocra."

Nuru looked from Breaker to Cleaver, and then back to Breaker again. Nuru sensed all the troopers thought the same thing, that it was a bad idea for him to become separated from the Breakout Squad. Although Nuru had not perceived any threats on the station, he did not dismiss the troopers' shared concern. Their job was to protect him, and their ability to do that would be limited if they were separated by even a short distance. Which was why they wanted Cleaver to go with him, not so much to serve as his translator but as his backup.

Nuru looked back at Veeren, whose eyes had never left him. Nuru said, "Yes, of course. My translator must join us."

The refurbished droid commando stepped up beside Nuru. Without taking her eyes off Nuru,

Veeren spoke in rapid Cheunh. Nuru was still wondering whether she had just made a short statement or asked a question when Cleaver offered an equally fast response. The only word Nuru caught was *crahsystor*, which meant *commander*.

Veeren's red eyes flicked to the droid and back to Nuru. She said. "Your translator will join us."

Nuru looked at the droid. "You both spoke so fast, I couldn't understand."

Cleaver replied, "Essentially, Aristocra Sev'eere'nuruodo asked if my commander could be trusted. And essentially, I replied that I trust my commander more than any other Chiss that I have ever met."

Nuru's mouth almost fell open. "You didn't!" he said, aghast.

The droid looked at Veeren and added, "I believe I pronounced every word correctly?"

"You did," Veeren said.

Nuru shook his head. "Aristocra, I'm sorry if you think my translator implied that he trusts me more than he trusts you."

"You should not be sorry," Veeren said. "Your mechanical translator's response was immediate and technically accurate. He is correct in that he has no reason to trust me. And had he expounded on your honor, I would have suspected he was engineered to promote you for political purposes."

"Oh," Nuru said, "I, uh, wouldn't have wanted you to suspect that."

She gestured again toward the doorway. Nuru and Cleaver followed her out, and the door sealed behind them. To the right of the door, the window remained open, allowing those still in the docking bay to see Nuru and Veeren sit in the conical seats while Cleaver came to a stop beside Nuru.

Peering through the window, Knuckles muttered, "Well, I guess now we know that Cleaver was right about something earlier. There is definitely *not* a Cheunh word for hospitality."

Breaker said, "Remember, fellas . . . different people, different customs. For all we know, that girl was being polite by Chiss standards."

"That may be," Sharp said, "but I can't say I like the way the Aristocra talks to Commander Nuru. She just seems . . . disrespectful."

Lalo Gunn had remained standing at the bottom of the *Harpy*'s landing ramp. Gazing through the window at the two seated figures, she said, "If you ask me, the Chiss girl has Nuru's undivided attention. Our little Jedi friend may not like her manners either, but he *wants* to like her. The way he looked at her and stammered, it was more than a little obvious. Chatterbox noticed it, too."

Breaker, Sharp, and Knuckles all looked at Chatterbox and said simultaneously, "Really?"

Chatterbox nodded.

Seated across from Veeren in the conference room, Nuru said, "Will anyone else be joining us?"

"No," Veeren replied firmly.

"Oh," Nuru said. He glanced at Cleaver, who stood beside him, then looked back at Veeren. He said, "It's just . . . well, I expected I'd be meeting more Chiss. Maybe because I sense there are others on board . . . watching us?"

Veeren remained silent for a moment, then said, "A security detail is monitoring this room and also the docking bay. You will explain your understanding of this meeting's purpose."

"All right," Nuru said, shifting in his seat, which wasn't very comfortable. "Chancellor Palpatine informed me that an ambassador of the Chiss Ascendancy contacted his office, requesting to meet with a representative of the Jedi Order. The Chancellor expressed his hope that this would be an opportunity to begin diplomatic relations between our governments. He assigned me to this mission because he believed you would be pleased to meet a Chiss Jedi."

"*Please* me?" Veeren said. "Your Chancellor assumes much."

Confused, Nuru said, "You . . . are disappointed?"

"Defense Force Station Ifpe'a is *not* a pleasure craft."

Nuru said, "I regret I am not communicating clearly. I believe the Chancellor, in sending me, hoped to show that Chiss are not strangers to the Republic. Would you have preferred a different Jedi?"

Veeren seemed to study Nuru's face, then said, "Although I thought I understood your language, I do not understand why you ask questions that reveal your ignorance."

Taken aback, Nuru said, "Well, I ask questions to gain knowledge."

"Your methods of diplomacy are very strange," Veeren said. "You would not object if I asked you questions?"

"No, not at all."

"What do you know of your heritage?"

"My heritage?" Nuru said, surprised by the question. "I . . . I am a Jedi. I was raised at the Jedi Temple on Coruscant."

"And how did you arrive at the Jedi Temple?"

"A Jedi discovered a Chiss ship's escape pod drifting in the Outer Rim. I was the pod's only occupant. I was an infant."

"And how did you come by the name *Nuru Kungurama*?" Her upper lip sneered slightly as she pronounced his name.

"According to the Jedi who found me, a data cylinder identified me by that name."

"What is the total firepower of your Republic fleet?"

"What?!" Nuru said, startled by the sudden change in course of the questioning. "I . . . I don't believe I'm at liberty to share that information."

Veeren replied, "You should be so cautious with *all* information."

Feeling as if he were incapable of saying anything right, Nuru glanced at Cleaver, who had been standing beside him in silence the entire time. Nuru said, "I don't suppose you have any data about Chiss protocol?"

"No," Cleaver said, "but if you need me to translate anything, let me know."

"Thanks," Nuru said. Looking at Veeren, he again tried to regain his composure. "With all due respect, Aristocra, I believe this meeting would be more productive if you explained why you requested a representative of the Jedi Order to travel to this station."

"Of course," Veeren said. "The Chiss Expansionary Defense Force has reliable sources throughout your galaxy. We are aware of the civil war between the Republic and Separatists, and that many Jedi are now in command of the Republic's armies. Twenty days ago, a cluster of unidentified spacecrafts was sighted near our borders before they escaped into hyperspace. I am compelled to—"

Nuru leaned forward in his seat. "Forgive me for

interrupting," he said, "but I believe I should have told you something earlier. During my communication with Chancellor Palpatine, he mentioned that the Separatists might have spies in Chiss space, which was why he proposed sending me on a classified mission to meet you. I imagine it's possible that the unidentified spacecraft belonged to the Separatists."

Veeren stared at Nuru for a moment, and then, completely ignoring his interruption, she continued, "I am compelled to inform the Jedi Order that our defense force has increased border patrols, and will not tolerate trespassers."

Nuru waited for Veeren to say more, then realized she seemed to be done. He said, "I don't understand. Are you implying that the unidentified spacecraft may have been . . . vessels carrying Jedi?"

"I am not implying anything," Veeren said. "I am *telling* you that the Chiss Expansionary Defense Force will not tolerate trespassers."

Nuru raised his eyebrows quizzically. "You want the Republic *and* Separatists to stay away?"

"Correct," Veeren said. "The Chiss Ascendancy has no interest in your war. If either the Republic or Separatists regards the Chiss Expansionary Defense

Force as a potential ally, it would be a grave error in judgment. You may leave now."

Nuru was stunned. He could barely believe that he had been encouraged to travel with the Breakout Squad so far across space, only to be dismissed by this Chiss ambassador and told to never return. He realized just how much he had hoped to learn about his native world and people, and with that hope dashed, his disappointment was almost crushing. *I really wasn't prepared for this mission,* he thought.

But he also remembered he was a Jedi.

Nuru took a deep breath to calm himself. Rising from his seat, he said, "I thank you for your time, Aristocra Sev'eere'nuruodo. I shall relay your message to Chancellor Palpatine as soon as—"

A muffled explosion interrupted Nuru. Veeren turned her head to the side and said, "Status."

From a hidden audio unit behind Veeren's chair, a disembodied voice replied, "Incoming."

"Incoming?" Nuru repeated as he and Cleaver turned to the viewport to see their allies beside the *Hasty Harpy.* The four troopers had heard the explosion, too, and had already unslung their blaster rifles.

More explosions sounded. Behind Veeren's chair, a section of wall slid back to reveal a wide viewscreen. Veeren's chair swiveled in the air, turning fast so she could face the screen, on which appeared the image of a black-uniformed male Chiss.

"We are under attack, Aristocra," said the officer from the screen. "An armada dropped out from hyperspace."

Veeren said, "Display."

The viewscreen shimmered. The officer's image vanished and was instantly replaced by the spectacle of more than a dozen warships and countless *Vulture*-class droid starfighters swarming the space station.

Nuru exclaimed, "Separatist fighters!" And then he sighted a bulky Metalorn yacht among the warships, and recalled that Overseer Umbrag of the Techno Union owned such a vessel.

The station shuddered violently as it was wracked by a more devastating series of explosions.

Watching the viewscreen, Veeren said, "They could not have arrived at this location by accident." She swiveled her seat to face Nuru, "Someone led them here."

CHAPTER 5

Nuru was astonished by Veeren's accusation. Before he could respond, the Chiss space station buckled under the force of a singular massive shockwave, and a loud, electric hum filled the air. The power of the blast sent Cleaver lurching backward across the meeting room. Veeren tumbled out of her hovering chair, which was left spinning in the air. Nuru braced his legs as he caught Veeren, turning his head fast to prevent her nose from colliding with his jaw.

"Let go!" Veeren said as she pushed herself away from Nuru. She staggered toward the viewscreen. Before she could reach it, the viewscreen made a crackling noise and fizzled off. A split second later, the meeting room and the docking bay were thrown into darkness.

In the docking bay, the troopers activated the tactical spot lamps on their helmets. While Chatterbox and Sharp trained their spot lamps on the surrounding walls and held their positions beside the *Hasty Harpy*, Breaker and Knuckles darted through the doorway that led to the meeting room.

Emergency lights flickered on, and the meeting room's viewscreen winked back to life. Veeren faced the viewscreen and said, "Status." The viewscreen flashed three times, then died again along with the emergency lights.

As Breaker and Knuckles raced into the meeting room, their spot lamps landed on Cleaver as he tottered back beside Nuru. "Who hit us?" Knuckles asked.

Nuru said, "Separatist warships!"

"Status!" Veeren repeated sharply. The viewscreen flickered again.

The electric hum grew louder. Out of the corner of his helmet's T-visor, Breaker saw the viewscreen brighten unexpectedly. Although he knew nothing about Chiss technology, his instincts told him that the station's energy systems were overloading, and that he wouldn't be able to warn the others fast enough.

"Down!" Breaker shouted as he launched his armored body between the viewscreen and Veeren. The trooper was still in midair when the viewscreen exploded. His armor took most of the blast as he wrapped his arms around the Chiss girl.

Breaker grunted as he hit the floor, letting his right arm and leg take the impact. He held the girl close against his chest, protecting the back of her head with his left hand as they rolled to a stop against the base of the wall.

Smoke poured out from the ruined viewscreen and began to fill the meeting room. Knuckles directed his spot lamp at the two figures on the floor. Nuru moved past the floating conical chairs, fell to Breaker's side, and said, "Are you two all right?"

"Never better," Breaker muttered as he carefully extracted himself from Veeren. But as he shifted his black-gloved hand out from under her head, she slumped against the floor.

Nuru felt his stomach clench. He moved his

hand to Veeren's neck, and exhaled with relief when he found a pulse. "She's alive!" As smoke continued to fill the room, he added, "We have to get her out of here. Now!"

Knuckles picked up Veeren while Cleaver and Nuru helped Breaker to his feet. They moved fast out of the meeting room and returned to the docking bay, where they found Sharp and Chatterbox waiting for them. Sharp asked, "Who's hitting us?"

"Separatist warships!" Nuru replied, and then he heard a loud crack from above. The docking bay's ceiling was buckling. "Where's Gunn?"

Chatterbox aimed a thumb at the *Hasty Harpy* as Sharp said, "Inside! Come on!" Sharp made sure everyone made it up the landing ramp, and then followed them in, just as the *Harpy*'s engines roared to life.

"Take care of the Aristocra!" Nuru shouted to the troopers as the ramp lifted behind him. The freighter's engines thundered louder. Nuru bolted to the cockpit. He came up fast behind Gunn's seat and said, "Gunn, we're under attack by—"

"Everyone on board?" Gunn interrupted.

"Yes, but—"

"No time for 'buts,' kid!" Gunn said as she flipped control switches. "It's time to leave!" She pressed a trigger and the *Harpy*'s laser cannon opened fire, punching a large hole in the docking bay's sealed door. The docking bay's air whipped out through the breach and into space. The *Harpy* lifted off the landing pad and began drifting toward the opening. Gunn made a quick adjustment to her cannon's control and fired again, expanding the hole.

"Gunn!" Nuru cried as he gripped the back of Gunn's seat. "There's a Separatist armada out there!"

"Too bad for them!" Gunn said. She moved both hands to the flight controls and launched the *Harpy* out through the gaping hole in the door. The *Harpy*'s tail had barely cleared the breach when the docking bay's ceiling collapsed, spraying debris behind the fleeing ship.

Droid starfighters were everywhere. Two fighters flew directly into the *Harpy*'s path and collided with her energy shields. As the Corellian transport bounced at the impact, Gunn activated the intercom and shouted, "Chatterbox! Cockpit! Now!"

Gunn sent the *Harpy* into a steep dive away from the space station and accelerated. Through the cockpit windows, Nuru sighted the Metalorn yacht amid the Separatist warships, then glimpsed dozens of small, cylindrical vessels streaking away from the station. Nuru assumed they were Chiss escape pods, and wondered if they were equipped with hyperdrives. He had his answer a moment later, as he watched all the vessels angle off in the same direction, and then rapidly vanish into space.

Nuru peeked at the sensor scopes and saw several droid fighters veer away from the station, moving in pursuit of Gunn's ship. A moment later, Chatterbox moved fast past Nuru and jumped into the seat beside Gunn.

Laser fire hammered at the *Harpy*'s aft shields. Gunn took evasive action, sending the *Harpy* into a controlled roll. She kept her eyes forward, not looking at Chatterbox as she commanded, "Enter an emergency transposal on our last jump into the navi-computer, just like I showed you how."

Chatterbox began pressing buttons on a console. Nuru said, "Emergency transposal?"

"That's right, kid," Gunn replied. "We can't outrun all those fighters, and we're in the *Unknown* Regions, remember? Our only chance of escaping this mess is through hyperspace, and the only route the navi-computer has for this area is back the way we came!"

"But that'll take days!" Nuru protested.

"We don't have a choice!" She activated the ship's intercom and said, "Everyone hang on, we're gonna jump!"

The *Harpy* swerved around another group of fighters, then shuddered as more laser fire pounded at her shields. Nuru sank his fingers deeper into the back of Gunn's seat and said, "How long before we jump?"

"We'd be doing it faster if your blue girlfriend had given us alternative routes to choose from!"

Another hail of laser fire streaked passed the cockpit. Looking at the back of Gunn's head, Nuru said, "Huh? Girlfriend?!"

Ignoring Nuru, Gunn snapped, "Is the navi-computer set?!"

Three agonizing seconds past as Chatterbox studied a technical readout, then turned to Gunn and gave her a thumbs-up.

Gunn asked, "Where's the portal?"

Chatterbox pointed to a winking yellow spot on

the navigational scope. Gunn glanced at the scope, saw the portal's location, and angled toward it. As they neared the portal, Gunn said, "Punch it!"

A droid fighter swooped in front of the *Harpy*. Gunn swerved to avoid hitting the fighter at the same time that Chatterbox pulled back on the lightspeed throttle. An instant later, the *Harpy* launched into hyperspace.

As the view through the cockpit windows transformed from distant points of light to long, brilliant streaks, Nuru gasped. "We made it!"

Gunn laughed. "That was a close one, all right."

"You said it," Chatterbox agreed.

Gunn punched Chatterbox in the arm. She said, "There you go, mouthing off again!" She glanced back at Nuru and said, "Go tell the others that we're in for another long trip."

Eager to check on the Aristocra, Nuru left the cockpit and went to the main cabin. As he ducked through the connective passage tube, he was wondering if Veeren was still unconscious when he heard a voice that gave him the answer.

"Where am I?!"

Stepping into the main cabin, Nuru found Veeren lying on the acceleration couch, with Knuckles and Sharp crouched on the deck beside her. Knuckles had strapped Veeren to the couch for her own safety during their hasty escape from the station. Now awake, she wriggled against the restraints. On the other side of the cabin, Cleaver stood beside Breaker, who had removed his helmet but remained seated.

Veeren freed one of her arms and tried to strike Sharp. Knuckles grabbed her wrist and said, "Hold still!"

"Release me at once!"

"We're trying to!"

"Aristocra," Nuru said firmly as he stepped closer to her, "please, be calm."

Veeren twisted her head to face Nuru. Her red eyes burned at him.

"Your viewscreen exploded in the conference room," Nuru said. "There was a lot of smoke, and the docking bay was collapsing. We had to get you out of there. You might have been killed if not for the quick action of this trooper."

He gestured to Breaker, who shifted in his seat while Cleaver helped him peel off his armor. Facing

Breaker, Nuru said, "Are you all right?"

"Just a scrape," Breaker said. "But I need a fresh bacta patch for my ribcage." He turned to Cleaver, who handed him a medpac.

Nuru returned his attention to Veeren. As Knuckles and Sharp removed the straps that had held the girl in place, she sat up on the couch and glanced around the cabin's interior, taking in her surroundings.

"You're on our ship," Nuru said. "Your station was still under attack when we escaped." Turning back to Breaker, he said, "I saw a Metalorn yacht among the warships."

Breaker scowled. On Kynachi, he had witnessed Overseer Umbrag's escape from the planet on a Metalorn yacht. He said, "You think Umbrag led the attack?"

"I can't be certain. But how did he obtain the coordinates to reach the space station?" Nuru wondered. Turning to Gunn, he asked, "Could he have followed us through hyperspace?"

Before Gunn could answer, Veeren interrupted, "Return me to Defense Force Station Ifpe'a at once."

"I regret that's impossible," Nuru said, "and not just because I don't know whether your station was completely destroyed. We're currently traveling through hyperspace on a preset course. It was the only way we could escape the assault. Apparently, your comrades chose the same method to evacuate. I saw many escape pods jettison from the station. It looked like all of them made it into hyperspace."

Through clenched teeth, Veeren said, "What is your course?"

Nuru knew that Veeren would not like his answer, and he felt his throat go dry. "The only navigational coordinates we had for this journey were the ones we used to reach your station, so we executed an emergency transposal to backtrack to our previous jump. If the hyperlane we're presently traveling has a name, we weren't informed of it, but I could show you our approximate position on a star map."

"That won't be necessary," Veeren said. "You will do whatever you can to return me to Chiss space at once. If you do not, the ruling families of the Chiss Ascendancy will learn of the attack on Station Ifpe'a, and will assume that the Galactic Republic and the Separatist Alliance have joined forces against the

Chiss. Your Chancellor will be notified that the Ascendancy acknowledges the attack as a declaration of war."

"What?!" Nuru gasped. "But we were *all* victims of the Separatist attack."

Veeren closed her eyes, held them shut, and then opened them slowly, her gaze now directed at the empty area of the deck between her and Nuru. She said, "I am Aristocra Sev'eere'nuruodo of the Second Ruling Family of the Chiss Ascendancy. You will receive no other information from me as long as you hold me captive."

"Captive?" Nuru said. "Aristocra, we aren't holding—"

Veeren's eyes flicked to Nuru's face, and her expression was so severe that it silenced him at once. "I am Aristocra Sev'eere'nuruodo," she repeated, "of the Second Ruling Family of the Chiss Ascendancy."

Nuru could not recall ever having met anyone who frustrated him as much as Veeren. He took a deep breath, exhaled slowly, then looked at Sharp and Knuckles. "The Aristocra is not our prisoner," he said. "Make sure she's comfortable. But keep an eye on her and don't let her touch anything. For all we know, *she's* responsible for luring the Separatist attack on her own station."

"That's ridiculous!" Veeren snapped.

Nuru, the three troopers, and Cleaver looked at Veeren. She realized that she had failed to remain silent, and she lowered her gaze to the deck.

Nuru wasn't sure, but he thought he saw Veeren's cheeks flush to a slightly deeper shade of blue.

Knuckles noticed Veeren's color change, too, and muttered, "Is there a Chiss word for *embarrassed*?"

Nuru kept his gaze on Veeren. Using the Force, he sensed that she was not only flustered, but also angry. And frightened.

"Aristocra," Nuru said, "you have made it clear that you don't trust me. If you choose to remain silent, I doubt our relationship will improve. Still, you have my promise that we shall make every effort to return you to Chiss space as soon as possible. And I want very much to assure you that neither I nor anyone aboard this ship alerted the Separatists to your station's location."

Veeren looked up at Nuru. She said nothing. Nuru assumed she was ready to listen.

"As I understand the facts," Nuru continued, "you provided the navigational coordinates to Chancellor Palpatine, and he relayed them directly to us. The Chancellor expressed concern over the possibility of Separatist spies in Chiss space, and you maintain that unidentified spacecraft were recently sighted near your borders. If you transmitted the coordinates to the Chancellor, is it possible that the Separatists intercepted the transmission?"

Veeren pursed her lips, then replied, "I am Aristocra Sev'eere'nuruodo of the Second Ruling Family of the Chiss Ascendancy."

Nuru grimaced, then shook his head sadly. Tearing his gaze away from Veeren, he looked to Knuckles and Sharp. "We have a long ride ahead of us," he said, "I'm going to the cockpit. Don't let the Aristocra out of your sight."

He turned for the passage tube and was about to exit the main cabin when he sensed another emotion radiating from the Chiss girl who remained seated on the couch, watching his back. The emotion was so intense that he came to a dead stop.

She hates me.

He turned and looked back at Veeren. Red

eyes ablaze, her expression might have appeared unchanged to the troopers, but Nuru felt the difference, an increased tension in the air. She radiated fury.

Nuru's brow furrowed, and then he turned away and proceeded into the passage tube. He wondered why Veeren hated him. He doubted there was any point in asking.

An alarm blared in the cockpit, waking Nuru. He had fallen asleep in the copilot's seat, which Chatterbox had vacated so Nuru could get some rest and also keep his distance from Veeren, who remained in the main cabin. Nuru sat up fast and straight, and looked at Gunn just as she was slapping the alarm off. He said, "What's wrong?"

Gunn was in her own seat. Keeping one hand on the flight controls and both eyes at the luminescent flow of hyperspace outside the cockpit, she said, "We're gonna exit."

Surprised, Nuru automatically buckled his safety belt as he turned his head to examine a navigational readout. According to its inset chronometer, almost ten hours had passed since the *Hasty Harpy* had left Chiss space. He said, "We're not supposed to exit for another three *days*!"

Gunn activated the intercom and shouted, "Everyone hang on! We're dropping out!"

The *Harpy* shuddered. Nuru's safety belt bit into his lap as the freighter practically tumbled out of hyperspace. The hyperdrive automatically winded down at the same moment that the sublight engines kicked on. One of the sensor scopes emitted a loud burst of static. Outside the cockpit, distant stars rolled into view, followed by the tendrils of a wide cloud of gas and dust. The *Harpy* had arrived at the edge of an interstellar nebula.

Gunn turned down the volume on the sensor scopes with one hand while she used the other to tap the flight controls, bringing the *Harpy* to what felt like a slow, hovering stop. Nuru realized he'd been gripping the rim of the control console, and he eased his grip as he gazed out the cockpit windows. Although the nebula dominated the view, he could see many distant stars as well as what appeared to be a nearby star. Despite his extensive study of astronomy at the Jedi Temple, which included memorizing stellar configurations, constellations, and nebulae from numerous vantage points throughout the galaxy, nothing outside the cockpit looked familiar.

Nuru said, "What star system is this?"

"Just gimme a sec, will ya?" Gunn replied as her hands danced over the controls, calling up a diagnostic readout as she glanced at a navigational scope. She cursed under her breath, then readjusted the scope and checked it again. "Well, the good news is we didn't suffer any damage."

Turning to face Gunn, Nuru said, "But where *are* we?"

"That's the bad news." Gunn made another adjustment to the scope. "I don't have the faintest clue, and the navi-computer doesn't recognize this sector, either. And just to top things off, radioactive interference is scrambling the sensors. The hyperspace compass is on the blink, too. We may be officially off the charts."

"But we must be somewhere on the route that the Chancellor provided. Right?"

"Don't make me repeat myself," Gunn said. "All I know for sure is how many hours we were in hyperspace, and that we're not back where we started, or any place we've been before."

Nuru glanced at the navigational scope, then said, "Can we do another emergency transposal to get us back to Chiss space?"

Gunn scowled. "If the last transposal failed to retrace our path, there's no tellin' where we'll wind up if we try again!" She shook her head. "This doesn't make sense. The transposal should have worked."

"You've done it before?"

"I've done *most* things before," Gunn said irritably. "But I've never fallen out of hyperspace at the wrong time!"

Nuru returned his gaze to the nebula, and realized the *Harpy* was drifting. A moment later, a dark void came into view at the edge of the nebula. Nuru's eyes grew wide. He said, "Maybe we didn't just fall out of hyperspace."

"What do you mean?"

"Maybe something pulled us out."

"Huh?" Gunn looked at Nuru. "What are you talkin' about?" She asked as she followed his gaze through the cockpit windows. Then she saw the dark void, too.

It was a black hole.

CHAPTER 6

"A black hole?" Sharp said to Nuru. "A real one?"

"No, a *fake* one, you lummox!" Gunn interrupted. "Of course, it's real! Are you sure your name isn't *Not-So-Sharp*?"

"Sorry," Sharp said. Gesturing to the three other troopers in the *Hasty Harpy*'s main cabin, he continued, "We learned about black holes during our training, but none of us has ever seen one before."

Gunn rolled her eyes. "Far be it from me to spoil your holiday, boys," she said, "but in case you didn't know—"

"Captain Gunn," Nuru said.

"—a black hole isn't exactly a tourist attraction, or a place to go for a—"

"Captain Gunn, *please*!" Nuru made a discreet gesture to the acceleration couch, where Veeren was seated. Cleaver stood beside Veeren, watching her. Veeren was staring at the deck. Nuru suspected she might be in a state of shock.

Nuru reached toward the wall and pressed a button. A panel slid back from the wall, revealing a viewscreen that displayed a periscopic view of the surrounding star system. Nuru adjusted the scope to bring the black hole to the center of the viewscreen. Shifting his gaze back to the troopers, he continued, "I believe this dark void is an intermediate-mass black hole. Obviously, we're outside the hole's radius, beyond the pull of its event horizon, or else the gravitational forces would have crushed us already. However, the hole's radiation seems to have rendered the *Harpy*'s sensors useless. We can't determine our precise distance from the hole, or even measure its gravitational radiation. That's really all we know about our present position."

Breaker said, "Commander, do you think the black hole's gravity yanked us out of hyperspace?"

"It's certainly possible," Nuru said. "What's puzzling is that we were supposed to be on a transposal course, heading back the same route through hyperspace that delivered us to Chiss space. But if we're on the exact same route, we should have bypassed this sector without any difficulty."

"In other words," Gunn said as she moved beside Chatterbox, "it's highly likely that we left Chiss space on an altogether different hyperlane. Don't ask me how *that* could've happened, because I really don't know. Chatterbox entered the transposal commands correctly, just like I taught him."

Looking at Gunn and Chatterbox, Nuru said, "Right before we made the jump from Chiss space, we swerved to avoid hitting a droid starfighter. Did that cause us to enter the hyperspace portal at the wrong angle? I mean, would that have altered our course?"

Gunn chuckled. "I don't know how much you know about navi-computers," she said, "but mine's a top-of-the-line Microaxial. We could've approached the portal from any angle and our approach vector would have been automatically corrected."

Nuru considered what Gunn had said, then

responded, "Are you absolutely certain that we won't return to Chiss space if we try another transposal?"

Gunn shrugged. "We might return to the vicinity of the space station, or what's left of it. But given our proximity to a black hole in the Unknown Regions, and the fact that the navigational sensors aren't working, we might wind up heading straight into the black hole instead. All bets are off."

The group was silent for a moment as they contemplated their situation, then Knuckles said, "If we didn't travel back the same way we came, is it possible we're still in Chiss space?"

Nuru lifted his eyebrows. "Good question," he commented. "But there's only one person on board who might know the answer." He looked again at Veeren, and the others followed his gaze.

Veeren continued to stare at the deck.

"Aristocra," Nuru said as he stepped toward the seated girl, "if you've been listening, then you're aware that we're in a very unexpected predicament. If you have any knowledge of black holes in Chiss space, or of a specific black hole within ten hours of travel through hyperspace from your—"

Nuru was interrupted by a noise like thunder

at the same moment that the *Harpy* was struck by a violent shock wave. Everything that wasn't bolted down within the cabin's interior went flying. Nuru fell toward Veeren, but stopped short when his chest met a length of metal. It was Cleaver's arm, which had lashed out to catch Nuru. Cleaver swung Nuru onto the couch beside Veeren, who held tight to her safety belt.

Gunn and the troopers had been knocked off their feet. The troopers rose fast, reaching for any surface area that provided a grip or traction. Gunn scrambled up from the deck and glanced at the viewscreen that Nuru had activated. On the viewscreen, bright lights streamed past and burst against the *Harpy*'s shields.

Gunn shouted, "Chatterbox! Move it!" She darted into the passage tube that led to the cockpit. Chatterbox raced after her.

Another explosion. Another shock wave. The remaining troopers had braced themselves for the impact, but ducked as various bits of debris sailed and bounced across the cabin's interior. Cleaver clutched at the side of the couch while he adjusted his body to shield both Nuru and Veeren from the debris.

"Stay with the Aristocra!" Nuru shouted at Cleaver as he vaulted past the droid and into the passage tube. A third explosion launched Nuru against the tube's curved ceiling. Twisting his body as he returned to the deck, he landed on his feet and sprinted to the cockpit.

Moving up behind Gunn and Chatterbox, Nuru gazed past their shoulders and through the cockpit windows to see three starships hovering close to the *Harpy*. He immediately recognized two long, needle-like ships as old Vangaard Pathfinders, and was fairly certain that a saucer-shaped vessel was an Ugor salvage ship.

Three small starfighters whipped past the *Harpy*'s cockpit. Nuru didn't recognize any of them, but the third passed so closely that he involuntarily flinched. Before he could comment, yet another ship, an armored frigate, came into view, moving ominously into position directly above the *Harpy*. Nuru guessed its length to be at least two hundred meters. The frigate resembled a massive hammer attached to an assortment of thrusters, and it moved at a sidelong angle, displaying its portside hull. The hull was blistered with turbolaser emplacements and quad batteries, and all were aimed at the *Harpy*.

Nuru said, "Pirates."

"Ya think?" Gunn said. "I wonder if they speak Basic."

Four more starfighters swooped past the cockpit. Nuru leaned past Gunn and looked at the scopes. From what he could see, the *Harpy*'s sensors were still only picking up static signals, but a moment later, the commo board sounded with a general override broadcast. "Attention, Corellian transport!" a deep voice erupted from the comm. "Shut down your engines, lock all systems except commo, and prepare to be boarded."

Gunn muttered, "They *do* speak Basic."

"If you are carrying blasters," the deep voice continued, "leave them in your cockpit. If you attempt to escape, we will open fire."

"Stang!" Gunn cursed as she brought her fist down on the edge of the commo board. "I'm getting pretty sick of people telling me to shut down my weapons!"

Nuru craned his neck back to look at the freighter overhead. "With all the firepower they have trained on us, and our lack of navigational sensors, I don't think we have much choice."

Gunn cursed again as she shut down energy to the *Harpy*'s laser cannon. Nuru's mind began racing, trying to think of a way to protect Veeren and everyone else on board. Looking at Gunn, he said, "You've dealt with pirates before?"

Gunn chuckled. "Hasn't everyone?"

"Can you think of any way to keep them off the *Harpy*?"

"No," Gunn said truthfully, "but I might be able to stall them."

"Then do it!"

Without hesitation, Gunn pressed a button on the commo board. Adopting a nervous tone, she replied, "Oh, thank goodness you answered our distress signal! Do you have a tech droid who can fix a reactor leak and a—"

Gunn interrupted herself by pressing a switch to break the connection. "That ruse should buy us a few minutes," she said as she leaned away from the commo. "If they think the ship is contaminated, they'll send over a droid or some other loser first." She reached down to remove the compact blaster pistol that she kept in her right boot, got up, and placed the pistol on her seat. "Let them find at least one blaster, and they won't look too hard for others."

Nuru said, "I'm not leaving my lightsabers,"

"I didn't expect you would," Gunn said. "C'mon, you two." She moved past Chatterbox and Nuru, heading into the passage tube.

"We can't let them take the Aristocra," Nuru said as he followed Chatterbox and Gunn to the main cabin. "Is there any place she can be concealed?"

"Nowhere they wouldn't find her eventually," Gunn said.

They entered the main cabin, and found Breaker, Sharp, and Knuckles fully suited in their armor, holding their blaster weapons ready. Cleaver stood beside Veeren, who remained seated and wore a stern expression as she looked at the cabin's viewscreen, on which the enemy ships were visible. Breaker said, "What's the situation, Commander?"

"We're surrounded by pirates," Nuru said. "At least four ships and seven starfighters. They've demanded that we surrender our weapons and prepare to be boarded. If I can talk with their leader, I might be able to negotiate for the safety of—"

"Negotiate?!" Gunn said. "With pirates? Forget that!"

Nuru asked, "What do you suggest, Captain Gunn?"

Gunn surveyed everyone in the cabin. "I know a thing or two about how pirates think," she said. "If we're all going to survive, the pirates have to believe each one of us is uniquely valuable, and not in any way expendable. But under no circumstances can they learn that Nuru is a Jedi."

"Why?" said Sharp.

Gunn scowled at Sharp. "Because pirates don't like Jedi, and our goal is to stay alive. Better to pretend we're willing to be friendly with them than try to defy them, at least at first. We just need to stick together. Unfortunately, there's one person on board that I'm not sure I can count on." Then she turned to Veeren and added, "You listening to me, little lady?"

Veeren lifted her gaze to Gunn, but remained silent.

"You're smart to keep your mouth shut," Gunn said. "Because if you think your 'I'm the Aristocra' routine will cut you any slack with pirates, you may as well jump out of the airlock right now. And if you do *anything* to endanger the rest of us, I will shove you out personally. Got that?"

Veeren swallowed hard, then said, "What do you want me to do?"

"Whatever I say." Gunn turned abruptly to face Nuru and the troopers. "The pirates will be here any moment. I'm certain they'll transfer us to one of their ships. Give all your weapons to Cleaver. Now!"

"But, Gunn," Nuru said. "I can't let anyone else have my lightsabers. It would be . . . irresponsible."

"Then you'd better do a really good job of looking like you're unarmed, kid."

The troopers handed their weapons to Cleaver. Gunn quickly issued additional instructions to everyone. When Gunn was done, Breaker sounded skeptical as he said, "Do you really think that will work, Captain Gunn?"

"We don't have time for another plan."

"On second thought," Nuru said as he handed Ring-Sol Ambase's lightsaber to Cleaver, "perhaps you'd better hold onto this one."

Less than six minutes after Gunn had given brisk instructions to everyone on the *Harpy*, one of the two Vangaard Pathfinders latched onto the *Harpy*'s starboard docking port with a loud clang. A moment later, the port's hatch hissed open, and a short, fishlike alien boarded the captured transport.

The alien's name was Robonino. He was a Patrolian, a bipedal amphibian with mottled mauve scales. He once had two bulbous red eyes, but a dark patch covered the ruined socket formerly occupied by his left. Wide fins projected from either side of his laterally compressed head, and two arms extended from his sleeveless spacesuit. His arms resembled cumbersome, vestigial wings with knobby-jointed fingers. He clutched a scanning device in one hand and a blaster in the other. A pack of equipment was slung across his back, and he moved with a shambling stride that suggested his legs had never entirely adapted to walking.

Robonino's right eye surveyed the passage tube, then looked to the small monitor on his handheld scanner.

Another alien, a tall, broad-shouldered humanoid reptilian, moved up behind him. Before Robonino could announce that his scanner had not detected any radiation leaks, the reptilian shoved him aside and snarled, "Outta my way, fish-head!"

The reptilian was a Trandoshan named Bossk. Clad in an ill-fitting yellow spacesuit, his bulky forearms jutted out from sleeves that were too short and too tight. His leggings ended just below his knees, exposing his thick-skinned legs and bare feet that ended in clawed toes. His long-barreled blaster rifle looked almost ridiculous in the clutches of his massive, clawed hands, which looked as if they would sooner break the weapon in half than fire it with any accuracy.

Bossk's wide nostrils flared. "There's no reactor leak on this junkheap! I only smell stinkin' humans!"

He moved forward without grace or stealth, his heavy feet clomping loudly through the passage tube. Robonino held both his scanner and blaster in front of him as he followed Bossk into the transport's main cabin.

The two aliens found Lalo Gunn standing in front of the cabin's acceleration couch. Her arms were raised with her palms exposed and fingers extended to show that she wasn't holding any weapons. Behind her, Nuru and Veeren were seated side by side on the couch. Both wore dark, grease-stained coveralls with blue blankets wrapped around their upper bodies. The coveralls and cape-like blankets had been the most immediately available things that Gunn could find for disguises. Nuru's coveralls had deep pockets, one of which concealed his lightsaber.

Bossk growled through his fanged maw, then repeated, "There's no reactor leak!"

"I fixed it," Gunn said. "And I left my blaster in the cockpit."

Without looking at Robonino, Bossk said, "Check it out."

As Robonino sauntered off into the passage tube that led from the main cabin to the cockpit, Nuru realized that he had been holding his breath. He exhaled quietly. Nuru was worried about what would happen if the pirates found Cleaver, who—at Gunn's instruction—had hidden himself along with most of the Breakout Squad's weapons in the *Harpy*'s engine room.

Facing Gunn, Bossk blinked his eyes and said, "So, you fixed the leak, huh?"

"That's right," Gunn said. "Right after I sent the distress signal."

Bossk blinked again as he cocked his head. He appeared to be weighing information within the narrow confines of his thick skull. Nuru remained relatively calm as he watched the Trandoshan, but he sensed Veeren go tense beside him.

"Distress signal?" Bossk snapped. "I didn't hear any signal!"

"I was hired to bring these two kids to their family," Gunn said, and began to gesture with her left hand to the seated figures.

Bossk reacted with surprising speed. Shifting his blaster rifle to his right hand as he moved forward, he grabbed Gunn's wrist with his left and spun her around, wrenching her arm up behind her back and turning her body so that they both faced the two Chiss on the couch. Adjusting his grip on his rifle, Bossk tilted its barrel toward Gunn's head as he looked from Nuru to Veeren. He let out a low hiss, then said, "I wonder what blue kids taste like."

"Before you chow down," Gunn said coolly, "you should know they're worth more alive. A *lot* more. Their parents are loaded." She looked at the rifle's barrel as if it were a minor annoyance.

Gunn had told Nuru and Veeren to pretend to be brother and sister, members of a wealthy family. She had also told Nuru not to reveal himself as a Jedi unless absolutely necessary. Nuru sensed that Gunn was nervous, and admired her for not showing it. Because of his Jedi training, he was not at all frightened by the menacing Trandoshan. He knew more than a dozen different ways to disarm and disable the fiend without even getting up from the couch. Despite his own confidence, he felt sorry for Veeren, who had begun to tremble.

Veeren's obvious fear did not escape Bossk. Keeping his hold on Gunn, he leaned closer to the Chiss girl and said, "Think you're worth more alive? Haw! *Nothing* beats a free lunch!"

Just then, Robonino reentered the cabin, carrying Gunn's blaster in one of his pockets. The Patrolian stepped over beside Bossk and held up the scanner so the Trandoshan could see it.

Bossk glanced at the scanner's small monitor, then his eyes flicked to Gunn's face. He said, "How many life forms on board?" Before Gunn could reply, he pressed the tip of his blaster against her jaw, then added, "And if you tell me any number different than four, you're dead."

Gunn said, "Do you mean how many *more* life forms on board?"

Confused, Bossk said, "Huh?"

"You asked, 'How many life forms on board?' But I don't know if you want me to include myself, the two kids, you, and your friend."

"I asked you how many *more* life forms are on board!" Bossk sputtered defiantly. "And fish-head's not my friend!"

Hearing this, Robonino's fins flared out on both sides of his head, and his good eye twitched as he glanced at Bossk. Robonino took a cautious step away from the belligerent Trandoshan.

"My mistake," Gunn said. "But you already told me the number."

"Huh?" Bossk said again.

"You discouraged me from saying any number other than *four*," Gunn replied. "And you're right. There're *four* more life forms."

"I *know* that!" Bossk sputtered. "I *asked* you to tell me where they are!"

Nuru sensed the Trandoshan had reached a

boiling point, and hoped that Gunn would not attempt to correct the dimwitted brute. He shifted slightly on his seat, moving his hand beneath the blue blanket that fell over his lap until his fingertips brushed against the side of his lightsaber. He no longer cared about sticking to Gunn's plan. If he had to reveal himself as a Jedi to save Gunn, he would.

But Gunn stayed remarkably calm. Ignoring the pressure of the blaster rifle's barrel against her jaw, she tilted her chin slightly in the direction of a nearby hatch and said, "The other passengers are in the secondary hold."

"I know where they are!" Bossk said. "Fishhead's scanner showed me. So now, you open the hold, and no funny stuff!" He jerked Gunn around. Bracing her like a shield in front of him, Bossk guided her toward the hatch while Robonino readied his own blaster.

As they moved closer to the hatch, Gunn said, "There are two things you should know about the four passengers in the hold."

"What's that?" Bossk said.

"First, they're unarmed Republic clone troopers. I've got them contained in a force field."

Bossk snorted. "You putting me on?"

"No," Gunn said as she palmed the hatch's opening mechanism. The hatch slid back, and Bossk gazed over Gunn's shoulder to see four armored troopers standing upright, lined up with their backs against a plastoid bulkhead.

Even though Gunn had mentioned the force field, Bossk failed to notice the sheet of pale blue light that stretched from deck to ceiling within the hold, separating him from the four motionless troopers. He reacted automatically, and typically without thinking, by rapidly swinging his blaster rifle away from Gunn's jaw so that its long barrel now rested on her shoulder. Holding Gunn like a shield and now using her shoulder like sniper saddle, he squeezed off five powerful shots at the troopers.

The rifle's noise was almost deafening inside the *Harpy*, and each shot caused Veeren to flinch. The fired bolts exploded into bright bursts as the energy field absorbed their impact, while all four troopers remained perfectly still. Bossk was about to fire more rounds when Gunn shouted, "Force field! They're behind a force field!"

Bossk noticed the four troopers had not budged

from their position against the bulkhead. "I *know* they're behind a force field!" he snarled. "I just wanted to make sure the field was working!"

Behind Bossk, Robonino nearly laughed out loud at the Trandoshan's ridiculous excuse. Unable to contain himself, the little Patrolian released what sounded like a gurgling cough.

Bossk held tight to Gunn as he swiftly twisted his neck to look at Robonino, who quickly pretended he was only clearing his throat. Bossk said, "The other pirates didn't believe me when I told them about the clones. If this ain't proof, I don't know what is!"

While Nuru wondered what the Trandoshan had said about the clones, the Patrolian reached to his own belt to activate a comm, signaling his allies that the transport was secured. A moment later, footsteps sounded as more pirates boarded the *Harpy*.

Nuru and Veeren sat still and silent as a dozen life-forms from as many worlds shuffled, lumbered, slinked, and slithered into and through the main cabin. The pirates included a long-tusked Pacithhip who walked on robotic stilts, a female Arcona in a dark green pressure suit, and a Sullustan with a tattooed head. The largest pirate was a hulking

Swokes Swokes, who had had to crouch-walk to avoid bumping his bulbous, sharp-horned head against the ceiling. Nuru wondered if any of the pirates knew how to return to Republic space.

Still in the Trandoshan's clutches, Gunn sized up the Swokes Swokes as he passed her. The Swokes Swokes's lidless eyes barely glanced at Gunn before he ducked into a passage tube that led to the *Harpy*'s freight elevator.

The Arcona looked at the occupants in the cabin and loudly announced, "This ship is now the property of the Black Hole Pirates!"

Gunn did not enjoy hearing this, but resisted her urge to give the Arcona a dirty look. The Arcona turned her anvil-shaped head to face Nuru and Veeren. Nuru immediately noticed the Arcona's eyes looked like glittering gold.

"Sit tight, kids," said the Arcona. "We're all going for a little ride. And if you behave, there may be a place for you among us."

The docked Vangaard Pathfinder's engine fired, and then the Pathfinder began tugging the *Harpy* to the frigate. Robonino returned to the *Harpy*'s main cabin, and then he and the Arcona headed off to the engine room. Watching their departure, Nuru grimaced. All he could do was hope that Cleaver could avoid detection. Gunn's plan depended on it.

There was a loud *thunk* from outside the *Harpy* as the pathfinder delivered both ships alongside the immense frigate. The Trandoshan finally released his grip on Gunn, and he shoved her back toward Nuru and Veeren. Gunn stumbled but recovered her balance quickly, and spun fast so she could keep her eyes on the reptilian lout.

Bossk aimed a thumb at the open hold and said, "How come the clones are just standing there like that?"

"Before you started shooting," Gunn said through clenched teeth, "I was about to tell you the *second* thing about those troopers."

"So tell me already!" Bossk snapped.

Without batting an eye, Gunn said, "They're defective."

CHAPTER 7

"Defective?" Bossk said. "What do you mean, the clones are defective?"

"It's kind of complicated," Gunn replied. "It might be best if I talked with your leader."

"As far as you're concerned," Bossk said, "*I'm* in charge around here. Now answer me! Defective *how*?"

Just then, Gunn noticed the Swokes Swokes as he reentered the *Harpy*'s main cabin. Facing Bossk, Gunn said, "You watch your mouth, buster! I'll have you know that some of my best friends happen to be Swokes Swokes!"

Overhearing this, the surprised Swokes Swokes

stopped and looked at the female human beside Bossk. Bossk was baffled by Gunn's outburst and said, "Huh?"

"You heard me!" Gunn said. "I don't know what you have against Swokes Swokes, and I don't care! Swokes Swokes are highly intelligent, so don't you say otherwise!" And then she pretended to notice the Swokes Swokes for the first time. Speaking in the Swokes Swokes native language, Swoken, she said, "Finally, a friendly face!"

Across the cabin, Veeren whispered to Nuru, "What did she say?"

"I don't know," Nuru whispered back.

The Swokes Swokes twisted his fleshy neck to look at the passage tube behind him. He saw no one in the tube. Turning back to face Gunn, he pointed a thick, clawed finger at himself as he replied in Swoken, "Me?"

Bossk watched in astonishment as Gunn reached out to take the Swokes Swokes' monstrous hand in her own relatively delicate grasp. "I'm Lalo Gunn," she said in Basic. "I'm captain of this ship, or *was* at least until a few minutes ago. I'm so relieved you found me and my passengers out here. Are you the leader of these privateers?"

Bossk looked from the Swokes Swokes to Gunn and said, "You think *he's* the leader?!"

The Swokes Swokes ignored Bossk, and his gaping maw pulled back into a wide smile that revealed long, uneven fangs. "I'm not the leader," the Swokes Swokes said. "I'm Mokshok, first mate to Cap'n Mcgrrrr."

In Swoken, Gunn said, "A pleasure to meet you, Mokshok."

"Hey!" Bossk snarled at Gunn. "Enough gibberish! I was talkin' to you!"

"Mokshok," Gunn continued in Swoken, "I'd like to talk with you and your leader about how we might work together." Giving a dismissive glance to Bossk, she added, "Maybe we could talk in private?"

"Hey!" Bossk roared so loudly that Veeren flinched beside Nuru. "I'm in charge here!"

Mokshok said, "Take a walk, Bossk."

Bossk glared at Mokshok and snarled, "You don't give me orders, you big—"

Mokshok launched a meaty fist into Bossk's face. The Swokes Swokes's knuckles carried Bossk's head straight into the cabin's wall, which it struck with a sickening thud. Mokshok disconnected his knuckles from Bossk's face, and then the Trandoshan's knees buckled under him and he flopped to the deck.

From across the cabin, Nuru sensed that the blow to the head had not killed the Trandoshan, but had merely knocked him out cold. Although he did not know what Gunn had said to the Swokes Swokes, he was fairly certain she had goaded them into fighting each other.

Mokshok beckoned to two other pirates and said, "Take Bossk back to the pathfinder and dump him in the infirmary."

As the two pirates carried the Trandoshan out of the *Harpy*, Gunn glanced at the wall, where the impact of the Trandoshan's head had left a deep dent. Returning her attention to the Swokes Swokes, she smiled and said, "Thanks, Mokshok. I don't know why that fellow said such unkind things about you."

"Bossk is a jerk," Mokshok said. "He only arrived in this sector a few days ago, but I've been just itching to punch his clock. Kept on bragging about what a big-time bounty hunter he was, and babbling about the Republic having an army of clones. You ever hear such nonsense?"

Both Gunn and Nuru realized that the pirates must have been operating in a very isolated region of space if they had never heard of the Clone Wars until Bossk's recent arrival. Gunn replied, "I can't tell you about Bossk's experience as a bounty hunter, but he was right about the clones. I happen to be transporting four of them. They're harmless now, completely immobilized." She gestured to the open hatch.

Mokshok stepped over to the hold so he could view the motionless troopers. He said, "Those armored suits . . . have people in 'em?"

"Yup," Gunn said.

"Mcgrrrr will want to have a look at these guys."

"You said Mcgrrrr is your captain?"

"That's right," Mokshok replied. "You'll meet him soon enough." Returning his gaze to Gunn, he smiled as he asked, "Where'd you learn to speak Swoken?"

"A friend from Makem Te."

Hearing the name of his homeworld, Mokshok

sighed. "What I wouldn't give to see Makem Te again."

"What's stopping you?"

Mokshok was about to respond when a male human entered the cabin. Clad in a broad, shaggy vest that made him resemble a furry creature, the man also wore a darkly mottled tunic, baggy trousers, and well-worn boots made of exotic leather. His face looked heavy but strong, marked by few wrinkles except for the creases at the edges of his twinkling blue eyes, which were so incredibly pale, they resembled ice. A mop of grizzled hair fell across his forehead, and silver whiskers bristled from his cheeks. Nuru could only guess the man's age as anywhere between thirty-five and sixty years.

Clicking his heels together, the man smiled at Gunn, gave a slight bow, and said, "I am Hethra Mcgrrrr, captain of the *Random Mallet*, and leader of the Black Hole Pirates."

"Lalo Gunn," Gunn said with a polite nod. "Captain of the *Hasty Harpy*, and I'd like it to stay that way."

"But of course you would!" Mcgrrrr replied brightly. Without offering any hint at his intentions, he looked around the cabin and said, "I haven't seen a Corellian YT-1760 transport in a long, long time." His piercing gaze fell upon Nuru and Veeren. "Crew or passengers?"

"Definitely not crew," Gunn said. "Just a couple of rich kids I was taking back to their family. I'm also transporting four Republic clone troopers to a reconditioning center."

Mcgrrrr raised one eyebrow. "Clone troopers?" Turning his gaze to Mokshok, he said, "That new fellow—the Trandoshan—was telling the truth? The Republic is at war?"

"See for yourself, Cap'n," Mokshok said, gesturing to the open hold.

Mcgrrrr stepped over to the hold and peered into it. Looking at the troopers who remained motionless behind the force field, he said, "They're alive?"

"Yes," Gunn said.

"What do they look like under those helmets?"

"Like very tough men. The problem with *these* tough guys is they're defective, which was why I was bringing them to a reconditioning center."

"What's wrong with them?"

"From what I was told, 'wrong' is a matter of

opinion. I'd be happy to tell you about them, but my first concern is the safety of my passengers."

Mcgrrrr grinned. "You're proposing some kind of bargain?"

"I would be, if I were in any position to bargain."

This answer seemed to please Mcgrrrr. He clapped Mokshok on the arm and said, "As my first mate as my witness, I declare that no member of the Black Hole Pirates shall bring harm to your young charges."

"That's only slightly reassuring," Gunn said, "given that a rather large Trandoshan was threatening me with a blaster rifle just a moment ago."

Mcgrrrr sighed. "Ah, that Bossk. I suppose it's my fault for even allowing him the choice of joining our ranks after he and Robonino arrived in a broken-down spaceship a few days ago. But let's not dwell on the past. We're all friends now, right?"

"Maybe," Gunn said. "Friends help each other, and I could use some help. I didn't expect to exit hyperspace here, and could use some coordinates to help me return to Republic space."

Mcgrrrr grinned again, then said, "We can talk

about how we might help each other *after* you tell me about these clones."

"All right," Gunn said. "You see, clone troopers are engineered to obey their commanding officers and Jedi generals, but they—"

"Jedi commanders?!" Mcgrrrr raised both eyebrows. "The Trandoshan didn't mention that! Do the clones have powers like the Jedi?"

Gunn was surprised by the question, as was Nuru, who thought Mcgrrrr sounded genuinely eager to know whether the troopers were Force-sensitive. Gunn shook her head, then replied, "They're strong and resilient, perfect soldiers. But no, they don't have special powers."

Mcgrrrr looked at Mokshok, and Gunn saw that they were sharing some silent communication, the kind exchanged by people who have worked together for many years. Mcgrrrr frowned, then said, "Sorry, Captain Gunn, I interrupted you. I believe you were about to tell me how these perfect soldiers aren't quite perfect."

Gunn said, "Yes, well, the clones are engineered to be obedient to their commanders. The problem with *these* clones is that they'll obey anyone."

"Anyone?"

Gunn nodded.

"Without hesitation?"

"They aren't the thoughtful types," Gunn said. "You give them a command, they'll do it. They're unarmed, totally harmless . . . well, unless they're told to do something that might bring harm."

Mcgrrrr looked again at Mokshok and said, "I don't know about you, Mokshok, but I'd like to see a demonstration."

"Really?" Gunn said, as if it had never occurred to her that the pirates would be interested in the troopers. "I could deactivate the force field, and—"

Mcgrrrr and Mokshok pulled their blasters out and casually aimed them at the open hatch. Gunn was surprised by the sudden appearance of the weapons.

Gunn said, "I thought we were friends."

"*We* are," Mcgrrrr said. "But I'm reserving judgment on the armored boys. Switch off the force field, but do it carefully."

"Sure," Gunn said. Keeping her eyes on the two pirates, she backed into the hold and palmed a switch on the wall. The force field vanished with a static buzz. Breaker, Knuckles, Sharp, and Chatterbox did not budge from their stance. She tapped Breaker on the shoulder and said, "Trooper One! Sit down."

Breaker dropped to the deck and crouched against the bulkhead.

Gunn rapped a finger against Knuckles's helmet and said, "Trooper Two! Stand on your head."

Knuckles bent at the waist, placed his gloved hands and helmeted head against the deck, and then kicked his legs up so that the bottoms of his boots were aimed at the ceiling.

Moving past the inverted Knuckles, Gunn tapped Sharp's shoulder and said, "Trooper Three! Jog in place."

Sharp began jogging in place. Gunn turned to face the pirates who remained outside the hatch and said, "He won't stop until someone tells him to or his legs fall off, whichever comes first."

While Sharp continued jogging, Gunn tapped Chatterbox's chest plate and said, "Trooper Four! Remove your helmet and hold it by your side!"

Chatterbox took off his helmet, revealing his swarthy features to the pirates. Gunn smiled at him and said, "Trooper Four! Say, 'Captain Gunn is the love of my life.'"

"Captain Gunn," Chatterbox said in a gravely tone, "is the love of your life.'"

Hearing this, Mcgrrrr and Mokshok responded with loud laughter.

Gunn threw a playful jab at Chatterbox's side and said, "You messed up, Trooper Four!"

"I think he was close enough," Mcgrrrr said. Without warning, he said, "Troopers One and Two! On your feet!"

Breaker sprang up from the deck at the same time that Knuckles lowered his legs to right himself, so the two troopers were now standing side by side.

"Trooper Three!" Mcgrrrr said. "Stop jogging!"

Sharp came to a sudden halt.

"Troopers One, Two, and Three! Remove your helmets!"

Breaker, Knuckles, and Sharp obediently took off their helmets, revealing that they were identical to the already unmasked Chatterbox. All four troopers wore blank expressions as they gazed at the two pirates.

"Impressive workmanship," Mcgrrrr said. "Were they engineered and replicated from scratch, or did the cloners use a template?"

"Template," Gunn replied as she moved away from Chatterbox, stepping through the open hatch to stand beside Mcgrrrr and Mokshok in the main cabin. "A bounty hunter. Jango Fett. Ever heard of him?"

"No," Mcgrrrr said.

Mokshok said, "They don't look so tough."

Gunn said, "You should have seen them when I picked them up at the military depot. They had more room to move around. They can do lots of tricks."

Mokshok glanced at Mcgrrrr and said, "The crew could use some entertainment, Cap'n."

Mcgrrrr nodded, then looked at Gunn. "Captain Gunn, I'd like to hear more about the war in Republic space. I invite you and your passengers to be honored guests on the *Random Mallet*."

"That's very hospitable of you, Captain Mcgrrrr," Gunn said warily. Gesturing to Nuru and Veeren, she added, "But these kids *do* need to get home sooner than later."

Mcgrrrr chuckled. "Oh, I think you should definitely plan on later."

"May I ask why?"

"Because I don't expect any of you will ever leave this sector."

Hearing this, Veeren gasped. She stood up fast, leaving Nuru on the acceleration couch, and said, "I am Aristocra Sev'eere'nuruodo of the Second Ruling Family of the Chiss Ascendancy, and you will return me to Chiss space immediately." Her words tumbled out rapidly, as if their sudden release would somehow protect her that much faster. Nuru did not need any Force powers to know that Veeren was very, very scared.

Nuru glanced at Gunn, and saw her brow furrow. Gunn had been very clear when she'd instructed Veeren to avoid conversation with the pirates. Gunn stifled her anger, but stared hard at the Chiss girl as she said, "Hush, Veeren, and let the grown-ups talk."

Mcgrrrr smiled gently at Veeren and said, "It's kind of you to share that information, my dear girl. But even if I understood your prattle about a ruling family, or if you happened to be carrying an enormous sum of credits, I'm afraid it wouldn't help you now."

Mokshok looked at the two Chiss and said, "It's

not our fault. No one can leave this sector, including us." Turning to Gunn, he added, "That's why I'll never see Makem Te again."

"I don't get it," Gunn said. "Your ships have hyperdrives, right?"

"Of course," Mcgrrrr replied.

"So what's stopping you from leaving?"

"See there?" Mcgrrrr said, pointing to the cabin's viewscreen, which still displayed the *Harpy*'s scope-view of the black hole. "The fact of the matter is . . . we're cursed."

"Mcgrrrr and Mokshok are taking the passengers to the *Random Mallet*," said the Arcona to the stilt-walking Pacithhip. The Arcona had just entered the *Hasty Harpy*'s engine room, where the Pacithhip was inspecting the mechanical and technological systems. Peering past the Pacithhip's shoulder, the Arcona said, "Ever seen a hyperdrive like that?"

The Pacithhip shook his head slightly, careful not to let his tusks strike any nearby machinery. "This is a custom job," he replied. "Some parts I don't recognize because they're new, less than ten years old. But that's an Isu-Sim motivator hooked up to what looks like a hybrid Avatar-10 and MT-5 drive, maybe a prototype. And see those regulators and power converters? They're hand-tooled. They'd have to be, or else none of these incompatible bits would work right. This transport isn't just a hot rod. It's what the mechanics at Fondor used to call a Hutt's Folly."

"Meaning what?"

"Meaning that whoever paid for all this may have had more money than sense."

"Maybe these components weren't paid for," the Arcona said. "Maybe they were stolen."

"Either way, doesn't really matter," the Pacithhip replied. "This could be one of the most powerful hyperdrives in the galaxy, but it wouldn't do us any good." The Pacithhip sighed. "Mcgrrrr might want to have a look at this unit before we start tearing it up for recycling. Come on, let's go."

The Pacithhip led the Arcona out of the engine room. Neither noticed the gray-metal droid who had neatly folded his body between the hyperdrive motivator and power converters.

Cleaver unfolded and rose to his feet. He carried a pilfered E-5 blaster rifle across his back and a shock-stick at his side. Edging around the reinforced engine mount, he reached behind a heat shield to recover the cargo sack that he had placed there earlier. The sack held four blaster rifles, four pistols, assorted grenades, and a single lightsaber. He picked up the sack, then stepped toward the engine room's hatch and listened carefully.

His auditory sensors detected at least three pirates still on the *Harpy*. One pirate was just outside the engine room, making tapping noises at an engineering console. While the pirate tapped away, Cleaver considered his next move.

Lalo Gunn had been certain that the *Harpy*'s passengers would be transferred to one of the pirate ships, and she had been correct. But before the pirates had boarded the *Harpy*, she had only had time to tell Cleaver to hide with the weapons in the engine room, then do everything he could to follow Nuru and the troopers and deliver the weapons to them within thirty minutes. Her final command—"And don't get caught!"—had hardly been necessary.

Cleaver waited inside the engine room's hatch,

listening to the pirates while he contemplated his mission. Inside the cold confines of his refurbished droid brain, his cogitative processors generated a possible concern. None of the members of the Breakout Squad had mentioned whether he should avoid killing any pirates.

Taking the sack filled with weapons with him, Cleaver stepped out of the engine room and saw the pirate who stood before the engineering console. The pirate was the short Patrolian, Robonino. Seeing the droid out of the corner of his bulbous right eye, Robonino's facial fins flared out as he moved fast for his blaster.

Cleaver moved faster.

CHAPTER 8

"We arrived in this sector the same way you did," Hethra Mcgrrrr said to his guests as he settled down into his seat. "We were on our way elsewhere—in our case, to the Delphon system—when our frigate fell out of hyperspace early and without warning. That was just over ten years ago. Back then, we were known as the Mcgrrrr Gang, which I still think has a certain ring to it.

"We immediately discovered that our hyperdrives no longer worked. At first, we thought we had technical problems. But eventually, we came to understand that it was the black hole that caused our plight. The hole not only wrenched us from hyperspace, but radiates gravitational waves that affect the curvature of spacetime itself, playing havoc on our navi-computers. Even worse, it emits a possibly unique radiation that effectively nullifies hyperdrive technology. Though we can travel at sublight speeds, it would take several lifetimes to escape the forces that bind us here.

"Unable to reach lightspeed, we've been mired in this nameless sector for more than a decade now, reduced to preying upon whatever odd vessel tumbles into our midst. For example, the heap that delivered Bossk and Robonino a few days back has already been scavenged to repair other ships. And though our fleet has grown and we've gained a new name, we will forever remain trapped here, where money has no value. And *that*," he said with finality, "is the curse of the Black Hole Pirates."

"Did you just say something?" Lalo Gunn shouted over the surrounding noise as she turned to face Mcgrrrr, "Were you talking to me?"

Mcgrrrr chuckled in response. "No, Captain Gunn. I was just yacking my head off."

Gunn, Mcgrrrr, Nuru, and Veeren were seated at the captain's table in the banquet hall on the

Random Mallet, the pirates' hammer-shaped frigate. The captain's table was near an enormous, circular window that offered a sweeping view of the black hole. Neighboring tables had been pushed aside to make room for the four Republic troopers, who were obeying every command from the dozens of boisterous pirates who encircled them.

The noise level made it almost impossible for anyone to carry on a conversation.

"Trooper Two! Jump up and down!"

"Look at him go! Hey, Trooper One! Walk on your hands!

"That's nothing! Watch this! Trooper Three! Lift that crate!"

"Trooper Four! Stop Jumping!"

"No, you fool! It's Trooper *Two* that's jumping! Four's the one climbing the wall."

"Trooper Four! Do a backflip off the wall and land on this table!"

"Haw! He did it! Trooper Four, now do a—"

"Shut yer yap! It's my turn to boss one around!"

"Trooper One! Over here!"

Nuru had been able to hear Mcgrrrr's tale, and

had listened attentively. Nuru noticed Mcgrrrr was grinning, and had the distinct impression that the pirate's leader enjoyed watching his crew having fun. Then Nuru glanced at Veeren, who sat to his left, staring sullenly at the food that had been placed in front of her.

Nuru returned his attention to Mcgrrrr, who gave him a conspiratorial wink. Mcgrrrr leaned closer to him and said, "You and your sister ever think about becoming pirates, lad? Because if you have, today's your lucky day."

Nuru grinned sheepishly, as if the possibility intrigued him. "I can't say I've ever considered it, sir," he replied. "I . . . That is . . ." He gestured to Veeren, then continued, "Our parents expect us to become diplomats."

"Diplomats?" Mcgrrrr slapped the table. "What an amazing coincidence! My first mate, Mokshok, used to be a diplomat. He was an ambassador of Makem Te. From what I've heard, he was a good one, too, not that he enjoyed it very much. Endless conferences and private meetings. Too many customs to remember. Always having to dress properly. But look at him now!"

Nuru followed Mcgrrrr's gaze to see Mokshok howling with laughter among the other pirates who had gathered at the center of the banquet room. The pirates were singing and clapping their hands while the troopers performed the latest request, a high-kicking dance.

"Even with a black hole as a captor," Mcgrrrr said, "a pirate's life is a merry one. A life to be envied. What do you say, lad?"

"They all certainly appear to be happy and healthy," Nuru replied. "But when you mentioned that you prey on 'odd vessels' that fall out of hyperspace, I couldn't help wondering . . . Does *everyone* that you capture agree to join your gang?"

"I'm proud to say only two arrivals refused to enlist. A pair of Sullustans with strong feelings against pirates."

Nuru felt a sense of dread as he asked, "What happened to them?"

"We took them all to a small world not far from here. Helped them set up their own little camp, we did. Despite their aversions to piracy, they still manage to serve us in their own way. Raising crops, preparing provisions, helping with ship maintenance and whatnot. After all, they need *something* to keep them occupied."

"And what do they get in return?"

Mcgrrrr took a sip from a large goblet, then replied, "For one thing, they get to live, lad. They also get to do research on an ancient—"

"Who hit me?!" bellowed a voice so loud that the singing pirates ended their song and turned to see the speaker. It was Bossk.

The Trandoshan stood in the room's main hatch. He had one hand pressed against the side of his head and his other hand gripped his blaster rifle. Bossk glowered at the pirates, but then noticed the four armored Republic troopers who had their arms linked around one another's shoulders and were kicking their legs up in what seemed to be some kind of dance. Temporarily forgetting his aching head, Bossk growled, "What in blazes is going on?"

"A party, Bossk," Mcgrrrr replied. "We're welcoming some new additions to our ranks." Gesturing to an empty seat beside Gunn, Mcgrrrr added, "Won't you join us for a drink?"

"I wanna know who hit me!" Bossk said. "And why are those clones dancing?!"

"Because no one told them to stop," Mokshok replied as he stepped away from the other pirates so Bossk could see him. Keeping his lidless eyes on Bossk, Mokshok said, "Troopers One, Two, Three, and Four! Stop dancing and stand at attention!"

The troopers immediately drew their arms away from one another's shoulders and came to a sudden stop. Still facing Bossk, Mokshok continued, "These clones do whatever they're told. If you were more like them, you might not have wound up in the infirmary."

Bossk responded with a wheezing laugh. "That a fact? Seems to me you should be glad I'm not like them."

"Why's that?"

"Because I usually only kill for money. But those guys . . ." He tilted his chin toward the troopers. "The only thing stopping *them* from tearing your ugly head off is no one's asked them yet." Bossk's eyes flicked to the troopers as he barked, "Hey, soldier boys! Wanna have some *real* fun?"

The pirates who had regarded the four troopers as obedient, acrobatic servants suddenly imagined their violent potential. Then the pirates glanced at one another, and began backing away cautiously from the troopers.

Nuru noticed several pirates had moved their hands toward their holstered blasters. He glanced at Gunn and sensed her anxiety, that she was wondering the same thing he was. *Where's Cleaver?*

Bossk looked at the four troopers and wheezed laughter again. Returning his gaze to Mokshok, he said, "Lookin' a little worried there, friend. See, if I were you, I'd be thinking the best use for a bunch of clones is target practice."

Bossk began to raise his blaster rifle.

Nuru sprang from his chair, leaping high into the air.

Bossk stopped raising his rifle, holding it so its barrel was aimed at one of the troopers.

Nuru gracefully executed a midair somersault as he snatched his lightsaber from the pocket in his coveralls and thumbed the activator switch, igniting its blade with a loud hum.

Bossk's thick Trandoshan finger flexed against the rifle's trigger.

Still airborne and with his lightsaber blazing, Nuru angled his legs and positioned himself to land in front of the troopers.

Bossk's weapon fired, launching an energy bolt at the nearest trooper.

Nuru was still descending to the banquet hall's deck as he swung his lightsaber to slam the energy bolt back at the Trandoshan. The bolt smashed into Bossk's rifle, shattering it instantly and knocking it from Bossk's grip.

As Bossk's rifle clattered against the deck, Gunn jumped up from Mcgrrrr's table and ran to Nuru's side. She was still running toward him when Nuru saw a nearby pirate draw a blaster pistol.

Holding tight to his lightsaber with his left hand, Nuru extended his right hand as he used the Force to snare the pistol, yanking it from the startled pirate's fingers. The pistol sailed through the air toward Nuru and into his waiting hand. He immediately tossed the pistol to Gunn, who caught it just before she arrived at his side.

The pirates gaped in astonishment at the sight of Nuru's lightsaber. Gunn shifted her body behind Nuru so her back was up against his. Gunn said, "Maybe my plan wasn't such a good idea after all."

"*Now* you tell me," Nuru muttered. He scanned

the pirates who stood before him. As his lightsaber hummed, he said, "Drop your weapons, and surrender at once."

"Jedi?!" Mcgrrrr gasped as he rose from his seat. "The boy is a Jedi?!"

Wheezing laughter came from Nuru's left. He glanced at Bossk, who stood with his arms braced across his chest. When the Trandoshan was done laughing, he said, "Surrender to you, blue-boy? Ha! Just hand over the laser sword, and I'll carve you up neatly *before* I eat you."

Nuru was about to respond when he noticed a dark, humanoid figure move low and fast behind Bossk. The figure appeared to be carrying a large bag as he darted for a shadowy alcove. The figure's arm lashed out, flinging the bag at a low angle so it sailed past Bossk, struck the deck, and slid toward the four troopers who had remained at attention at the center of the chamber.

All the pirates watched the bag slide to a stop near the troopers, then turned to the alcove to see the mysterious newcomer who had thrown the sack. The pirates cringed as a second lightsaber ignited in the shadows, but Nuru saw something else. A pair of bright white eyes glowed in the darkness above and behind the lightsaber.

Cleaver.

The pirates were momentarily fixated on the dark figure they assumed was a second Jedi, but then they heard ratcheting sounds from the chamber's center, and returned their attention to the troopers. The troopers had quickly emptied the cargo sack and now stood in a tight circle, facing away from one another, with their blaster rifles leveled and ready to open fire on the pirates.

"The troopers were only pretending to be defective," Nuru said. "Each one is an expert shot."

"Goody," Bossk said, gnashing his teeth as he prepared to throw himself at the troopers. "Let's dance!"

"No!" Mcgrrrr shouted so loud that even Bossk was surprised. Then Mcgrrrr looked directly at Nuru and said, "Obey the Jedi! No one even *thinks* of harming the Jedi or their allies!"

Bossk said, "Huh?"

"You heard the cap'n!" Mokshok said as he faced his fellow pirates. "Lay down your weapons! All of you!"

Nuru watched with amazement as all the pirates carefully removed their weapons from their holsters and belts and placed them on the deck. Then he glanced at Veeren, who was gazing back at him. He felt some satisfaction in seeing that she looked relieved. But then, Gunn said, "Don't trust 'em, kid. Pirates will trick you every time."

"It's no trick, I assure you," Mcgrrrr said as he stepped away from his table, raising his hands so Nuru could see they were empty. "The fact is that we have long hoped for a Jedi to arrive here, as we believe only a Jedi can help us escape the sector." Tears welled up in his eyes as he added, "You really *are* a Jedi, aren't you?"

Nuru nodded. "I am Nuru Kungurama. My friend in the shadows is a droid." Keeping his eyes on Mcgrrrr, he said, "Come on out, Cleaver."

Still holding Ring-Sol Ambase's lightsaber, Cleaver emerged from the dark alcove. Breaker said, "Good work, Cleaver."

"Thank you, Master Breaker." Remembering the Patrolian he'd encountered earlier, he added, "I should mention that I subdued one pirate and left him tied up on the *Hasty Harpy*. I hope I did the right thing. His permanent termination seemed unnecessary."

"I'm sure you used good judgment," Nuru said.

Mcgrrrr glanced at Cleaver, then looked back at Nuru and said, "A Jedi. How very fantastic." Then he looked at Veeren and said, "You're his sister. Are you a Jedi, too?"

Before Veeren could respond, Nuru answered, "She is neither my sister nor a Jedi. She is a Chiss ambassador under my protection."

"I only wish you'd identified yourself sooner!" Mcgrrrr said. He turned to Mokshok. "Set course for Plunder Moon!"

"Aye, Cap'n," Mokshok said.

Bossk looked from the lightsaber-wielding droid commando to the four Republic troopers. Then he shifted his gaze to the disarmed Black Hole Pirates and then to their captain, who was practically beaming at the Jedi boy. Shaking his head with disgust, Bossk said, "You're all screwy."

CHAPTER 9

"All right, Mcgrrrr," Lalo Gunn said. "You and your pirates are off the hook."

"I'm pleased to know it," Mcgrrrr said with a polite bow.

Gunn had just completed a thorough inspection of her transport to confirm that the dent made by Bossk's head in the cabin's wall was the only damage caused by the Black Hole Pirates. She had warned Mcgrrrr that if any part of her ship were broken or missing, she would not be pleased.

Gunn and Mcgrrrr were standing with Nuru, the four clone troopers, Cleaver, and Veeren in the *Hasty Harpy*'s main cabin. Robonino had been freed and released to the other pirates. Gunn's compact blaster was back in place inside her right boot, and Cleaver had returned Ring-Sol Ambase's lightsaber to Nuru. Nuru had changed out of his borrowed coveralls and was once again wearing his Jedi robes. The troopers had removed their helmets, and they watched Mcgrrrr warily.

The *Harpy* remained docked with the Vangaard Pathfinder, which in turn was docked with the *Random Mallet*. All the ships and pirate starfighters were traveling toward a small moon in orbit of a gas planet. Facing Mcgrrrr, Nuru said, "You say we're on course for Plunder Moon?"

Mcgrrrr nodded. "That's the name we gave to the world where we placed the two Sullustans who refused to become pirates. They arrived out of hyperspace about eight years ago. Did I mention these Sullustans are sort of historians?"

"No, you didn't," Nuru said. "What do you mean by 'sort of'?"

Mcgrrrr scratched his chin. "Well, they're more like scientific researchers. They say they study ancient artifacts to learn about long-dead civilizations. There's a name for what they do . . ."

"Xenoarchaeology," Nuru said.

"That's it," Mcgrrrr said. "Anyway, not long after we delivered them to Plunder Moon, they began exploring an ancient structure, a partially collapsed pyramid. Inside the pyramid, they found alien glyphs and technology. According to the Sullustans, these glyphs suggest the tech can only be activated by someone with Force powers."

Nuru's red eyes went wide. "Captain Mcgrrrr, have the Sullustans encountered any large, blue-skinned reptiles?"

"None that I know of," Mcgrrrr replied. "But I recall the glyphs had images of saurian creatures. Why?"

"Because from what you've described, the pyramid sounds like a Star Temple built by a reptilian species, the ancient Kwa. Their descendants are the Kwi, who still exist on scattered worlds."

Impatient, Gunn said, "What do a bunch of old lizards have to do with getting us away from the black hole?"

"Possibly everything," Nuru said. "Jedi scholars learned that the Kwa harnessed the power of the cosmos—possibly the power of the Force itself—

inside massive underground chambers that lay below the Star Temples. The Kwa used this power to travel the universe through planetary-based hyperspace portals that they called Infinity Gates, and designed the Star Temples to protect the integrity of these gates."

"Whoa," Gunn said. "Planetary-based portals? That's impossible. Everyone knows you can't hyperspace until you're free of a planet's gravity. There's no way you can do it from inside a planet."

"As *I* understand it," Nuru continued, "the Kwa may have also possessed powers that allowed them to control their technology. Only a few Star Temples have ever been discovered. The Kwa left behind ferocious monsters and many hidden death traps to deal with intruders."

"I haven't heard of any monsters or traps," Mcgrrrr said. "All I know is that the Sullustans say the ancient tech can only be activated by a Jedi. The way they tell it, the tech could allow a number of ships to make a hyperspace jump out of this realm."

Gunn looked at Nuru and said, "Is this true? Can you make this happen?"

Nuru glanced at Veeren, and then at the troopers.

He realized everyone was waiting and hoping for a positive response from him, as if their lives depended on it. He said, "Kwa technology is very powerful . . . but extremely dangerous. At the Jedi Temple, I learned of an incident that happened about nine years ago. A small Star Temple was discovered on the planet Ova. Evidently, Kwa Star Temples can be used not just for interstellar travel, but as weapons to direct powerful waves of energy, called *infinity waves*, across the galaxy. Shortly after it was discovered, another planet's Star Temple fired an infinity wave at Ova."

Gunn said, "What happened?"

"Ova was obliterated."

"Oh," Gunn said, raising her eyebrows. "So where does that leave us?"

Veeren cleared her throat, then said, "I do not mean to say this as a threat, Nuru Kungurama, but merely as a statement of fact. If I am not returned to Chiss space, the ascendancy may go to war with the Republic. It is not my wish for this to happen, yet the situation is beyond my control. If there is anything you can do to help us leave this sector, I will alert the ascendancy that it was the Separatists—not the Republic—that attacked Defense Force Station Ifpe'a . . . and I would be most grateful."

Nuru did not want to disappoint Veeren. He said, "I imagine I'll have a better idea of how to proceed after we meet the Sullustans, and they show me what they've found at the pyramid."

"You'll meet them soon enough," Mcgrrrr said as he gestured to the periscopic viewscreen. "We're descending to Plunder Moon now."

Even though the ancient stone pyramid was partially collapsed, Nuru thought it was an impressive sight. Its height was ten times longer than the *Random Mallet*'s overall length, and it loomed like an artificial mountain over the Sullustans' camp, several small structures that made up the only other architecture on the lunar surface. The pyramid's sharply angled peak was so high above the ground that it seemed to permanently stab the crimson sky, just as it had done for over one hundred thousand years. Nuru could not help marveling over the fact that the pyramid was so many eons older than the

Jedi Order itself, and that most of the edifice was still standing.

The Black Hole Pirates had undocked and landed their ships along with the *Hasty Harpy* on a wide stretch of rocky ground beside the pyramid. While Veeren waited with Gunn and Cleaver aboard the *Harpy*, Nuru descended the *Harpy*'s ramp along with Mcgrrrr and the four troopers, then walked toward the Sullustans' camp.

Because Mcgrrrr had referred to two Sullustans living on Plunder Moon, Nuru was surprised to see three emerge from one of the camp structures, which were arranged beside a large vegetable garden. Two Sullustans were adults, a male and female, both jowly-faced humanoids distinguished by big, black eyes and large, prominent ears. The third was a Sullustan child, who appeared to be about six years old, and held the adult male's hand.

Nuru glanced at Mcgrrrr and said, "You didn't tell me they were a family."

"You didn't ask," Mcgrrrr replied with a grin. "Their daughter was born a few years ago."

The Sullustans trotted cautiously over to meet the landing party. The adult male Sullustan, who had the largest ears, looked at Nuru and the troopers, then stared at Mcgrrrr.

"What's going on, you thieving devil?" he said. "Found some other unfortunate fellows who have no interest in working for you?"

Mcgrrrr laughed. "It's good to see you, too, Professor Groob. Allow me to introduce Nuru Kungurama, a Jedi."

The three Sullustans stared at Nuru, who was only slightly taller than Professor Groob. "Real Jedi carry real lightsabers. How about you?" asked the professor.

Nuru pushed back his robe to reveal the two lightsabers clipped to his belt. He said, "Do you require a demonstration?"

The adult Sullustans glanced at each other, then Groob said, "No! Please, forgive our skepticism!" Gesturing to his fellow Sullustans, he said, "My wife and colleague, Parv Dijj, and our daughter, Ulsee. Parv and I are . . . I mean, we *were* professors of xenoarchaeology at the University of Ketaris."

Parv Dijj said, "Imagine our surprise when we discovered a Kwa Star Temple here!"

"But we're all eager to leave and go home,"

Groob added quickly. "Will you help us, young Jedi? Will you?"

Nuru was taken aback by the earnestness of the Sullustan's request. He said, "I don't know how much you know about Kwa technology, but in the wrong hands, it's been known to destroy entire star systems."

Groob said, "If you're referring to the Star Temple on Ova, I dare say we know more than most."

"We *discovered* the Ova Temple," Parv continued with obvious pride, "and provided the report that notified the Jedi Council about its existence!"

Groob added, "If we hadn't traveled to Coruscant to deliver our report, we might have been on Ova when it vanished into infinity! Not that we were entirely lucky. We were on our way back to the University of Ketaris when our ship fell out of hyperspace and wound up *here*."

Nuru got the impression that the Sullustans were enjoying the opportunity to talk about their experiences. Turning his gaze to the pyramid, he said, "Captain Mcgrrrr said you haven't stumbled across any monstrous guardians or traps in or around the Star Temple. Is this true?"

Groob nodded. "On Ova, we found plenty of traps and barely escaped an attack by enormous whuffa worms. The Kwa used whuffas as guardians for their temples. But on this world, we've found only the fossilized remains of whuffas. The worst danger is collapsing rubble."

Parv nodded in agreement, then added, "Clearing a route through the pyramid to the stellar control station wasn't easy."

"You've seen the station?" Nuru said. "The activation controls are functional?"

Groob said, "I believe you'll find that all they need are a Jedi's touch."

"How do you reach the station?"

"We fly!" Groob exclaimed. "Mcgrrrr left us with a swoop, which we keep in that shelter over there." He faced Mcgrrrr, then continued, "You have our salvage ship. If you return it, we'll lead you through the pyramid's collapsed area. After that, we'll all fly down through the caverns to the stellar control station."

"You can't be serious," Mcgrrrr said, gesturing to the landed ships. "Are you suggesting we fly all these ships . . . underground? You must be mad!"

"Don't worry," Groob said. "The caverns are huge, with room to spare for your frigate."

"But where will we land?"

"At the stellar control station, of course." Turning to Parv and Ulsee, Groob said, "Gather our datacards and leave everything else. We're heading home!"

"Home?" said young Ulsee, speaking for the first time. "Really?"

Nuru, Mcgrrrr, and the four troopers watched the Sullustans trot back to their camp to collect their records of the archaeological dig. Breaker moved close beside Nuru and said, "The Sullustans make it sound like we have nothing to worry about."

"Indeed they do," Nuru replied without conviction.

The Sullustans returned, carrying sacks stuffed with datacards. Mcgrrrr escorted them to the saucer-shaped Ugor salvage ship, which was the Sullustans' rightful property. Mcgrrrr proceeded to the *Random Mallet*'s bridge, where he began issuing orders over the commo. Nuru and the troopers returned to the *Harpy*, where they informed Gunn, Veeren, and Cleaver about the Sullustans and the planned journey to the Star Temple's stellar control station.

Nuru was in the *Harpy*'s cockpit with Gunn and Chatterbox when they received Mcgrrrr's instructions. Gunn eyed the pyramid and said, "We're supposed to fly into that thing to make a hyperspace jump? That kind of goes against all of my better judgment." Glancing back at Nuru, she said, "You trust these Sullustans?"

"I sensed that they were sincere," he said.

"They'd better be," Gunn said. "Because if they're setting us up, I won't bother letting them live to regret it."

One by one, the ships lifted off the lunar surface. The *Harpy* and the pirate vessels followed the Sullustans' saucer around to the pyramid's far side, where the collapsed area had left a gaping hole. The Sullustans activated their saucer's powerful floodlights and then entered the hole, illuminating the passage for the others who trailed behind.

Gunn switched on the *Harpy*'s running lights as they descended into a cavern. From what Nuru could see of the surrounding rock walls that slid past the cockpit's window, the Sullustans had been truthful in their assessment of the cavern's size.

The cavern widened, and the ships proceeded into an enormous chamber with a wide, sloping wall. At first, Nuru thought it was a natural wall, but as they flew closer to it, he saw it was constructed with massive blocks of cut stone.

The Sullustans headed for a vertical break in the wall, and led the other ships into the chasm. The chasm emptied into an even more enormous chamber, at the center of which was a gigantic geodesic sphere that was sheathed in smooth hexagonal plates, which emitted an eerie white radiance.

Chatterbox said, "Look at the size of that thing."

"Button your lip!" said Gunn.

"It's the power station," Nuru said. He was amazed by the glowing sphere's immensity, and estimated its diameter at more than two kilometers. "Keep following the Sullustans."

The Sullustans maneuvered their saucer around the sphere to a slot that spanned the width of an entire hexagonal plate. As the ships neared the slot, Gunn realized it was an inset landing platform, wide enough to accommodate many vessels. She asked, "When did the old lizards build this place?"

"More than a hundred thousand years ago," Nuru replied.

"But it looks so . . . new."

The Sullustans entered the slot and landed. The *Harpy*'s thrusters kicked on and she touched down beside the saucer. Nuru said, "Keep the engines running, Gunn. I don't know what we'll find here, but I expect we may need to leave in a hurry."

Nuru was already heading out of the *Harpy*'s cockpit as the *Random Mallet*, two pathfinders, and seven starfighters hovered into the slot and settled onto the ancient platform. Stepping into the *Harpy*'s main cabin, Nuru found Veeren, Breaker, Knuckles, Sharp, and Cleaver staring at the periscopic viewscreen, which now displayed the Kwa-constructed landing area. Nuru said, "Knuckles and Cleaver, stay with the Aristocra. Breaker and Sharp, come with me."

Veeren said, "I wish to go, too."

"You should stay here," Nuru said. "It's safer."

"Please. I want to see this place."

Nuru glanced at Knuckles and Cleaver. "All right," he said. "We'll all go. But be prepared to return to the ship immediately on my order."

The three troopers donned their helmets and

checked their weapons as they escorted Nuru and Veeren down the *Harpy*'s ramp. Cleaver followed with his own blaster rifle. A moment later, Captain Mcgrrrr and Bossk emerged from the *Mallet*, and then Professor Groob climbed out of his saucer to join Nuru and the others on the platform.

Nuru was surprised to see Bossk, who had replaced his ruined blaster rifle with a new one, which he gripped tightly in front of him. Bossk's tongue darted back and forth between his teeth as he stared at Nuru. The young Jedi faced Mcgrrrr and said, "Why did you bring the bounty hunter?" He had to speak loudly so his voice could be heard over the sound of the *Harpy*'s engines.

"I won't bore you with details," Mcgrrrr answered. "Bossk is my new first mate."

"Mokshok had an accident," Bossk said.

"How unfortunate," Nuru said warily.

Mcgrrrr leaned closer to Nuru and said, "Don't worry about Bossk. He's just muscle. If we run into anything unexpected, he could be useful."

Professor Groob patted Nuru's arm and said, "The main controls are straight through there, at the end of the corridor." Groob gestured to a triangular doorway in a nearby wall, which was adorned with bizarre glyphs. "I believe I can show you how to operate the controls, but only you can open the gateway for a hyperspace jump."

"Just a moment," Mcgrrrr said. "Shouldn't we talk about where we're going to jump? That is, we . . . well, some of us don't want to jump just *anywhere*."

Nuru looked at Groob and said, "Can the controls be adjusted for specific coordinates?"

"Yes," Groob said. "That is, I *think* so."

"What?" Mcgrrrr said. "You don't know for certain?"

"Ha! I suppose you think I should pop into the nearest convenience store and buy an instruction manual for ancient Kwa technology?"

"But if you don't know, how can we be sure the station even works?!"

While Groob and Mcgrrrr argued, Nuru noticed that Veeren had stepped away from Cleaver's side so she could inspect a series of glyphs that were etched into the wall to the left of the triangular doorway. As Veeren extended her hand to touch the glyphs, Nuru sensed a sudden tension in the air.

"Aristocra!"

And then the wall exploded outward, spraying dust and rubble in all directions and sending Veeren sprawling back against the platform. Nuru was already running to Veeren's position as he saw what had shattered the stone wall.

The massive head of a giant whuffa worm lolled in the newly formed hole, flexing its maw to display the long, diamond-hard teeth it used for burrowing through densely packed ground. Then the whuffa thrust its muscular mass forward, writhing out of the hole so it was poised to strike Veeren.

Nuru sprang and landed beside Veeren's supine form. He had hoped to shove or pull her away from danger, but as he grasped her arms, the whuffa flexed its maw wider and dropped its head fast.

Nuru and Veeren were swallowed instantly.

CHAPTER 10

Veeren clung to Nuru as the giant whuffa lifted its head to let gravity pull the two Chiss down its dark throat. The stench was so overwhelming that Veeren almost gagged.

Holding tight to Veeren, Nuru felt a stinging sensation at the back of one hand as it slid across the monster's inner flesh, which was slick with digestive acids. The whuffa flexed its jaws again, allowing light to penetrate its roomy mouth. Veeren screamed.

Nuru yanked his right arm out from behind her and seized his lightsaber from his belt. Looking up, he extended his arm toward the whuffa's brain sac and was about to ignite his weapon's blade when two rapid blasts sounded from outside. A pair of energy bolts tore through the whuffa's body, spraying gore and narrowly missing Veeren's body.

Nuru realized someone had fired a blaster rifle at close range into the whuffa. The monster responded reflexively by closing its jaws and thrashing its bulk away from the direction of the shooter. The sudden movement cast Nuru and Veeren back into darkness and sent them deeper into the whuffa's gullet.

Sliding away from the brain sac, Nuru nearly lost his grip on Veeren as he braced his legs and back against the inner walls of the whuffa's mouth and activated his lightsaber. He drove the weapon through the creature's flesh, then swiveled his wrist.

The whuffa opened its jaws, allowing light to pour into its mouth as it erupted into a blood-curdling shriek. Sighting the brain sac again, Nuru winced as he plunged his lightsaber into it.

The whuffa was still shrieking as its entire body convulsed. Its cry ended a moment later as it collapsed upon the ancient landing platform. Nuru had no sooner deactivated his lightsaber when he and Veeren tumbled out of the monster's mouth.

Dazed, Nuru pushed himself up from the gore-slicked platform. He could see the *Hasty Harpy*'s aft section, but the whuffa's enormous corpse blocked his view of his allies and the other ships. As he helped Veeren to her feet, Breaker and Sharp ran around the whuffa to arrive at Nuru's side. Breaker said, "Are you two all right?"

"Barely," Nuru said as he wiped his hands off on the inside of his robe. Veeren was trembling but did not budge as Nuru lifted a dry edge of his robe up to her head and gently rubbed the muck from her face and hair. "Who shot the whuffa?"

"The Trandoshan," Sharp said as they edged around the dead monster. "The fool would have kept shooting but Knuckles grabbed his rifle."

They found Bossk standing a short distance away from Mcgrrrr and Professor Groob. Bossk was glaring at Knuckles and Cleaver. Knuckles was not only still holding Bossk's rifle but had it aimed at the Trandoshan's head.

"I was just trying to kill the thing!" Bossk sputtered. Then he noticed Nuru and Veeren approaching, and added, "Besides, if anyone's gonna eat the blue kids, it's gonna be me!"

Facing Bossk, Nuru said, "Return to the *Random*

Mallet immediately, or Mcgrrrr will be needing another new first mate."

Bossk looked at Knuckles and said, "My rifle. I want it."

"Forget it," Knuckles replied. "Start walking."

Bossk looked at Mcgrrrr. Mcgrrrr said, "You heard the man, Bossk."

Bossk's head jerked back, and then he made a hacking noise as he launched a spray of spit that spattered against Knuckles' helmet. Knuckles didn't flinch. Bossk let out a wheezing laugh as he turned and stalked back to the *Mallet*'s ramp.

Mcgrrrr looked at Professor Groob and said, "What's the deal? I thought you said the whuffas were extinct!"

Facing the whuffa's corpse, Professor Groob shook his head, which made his large ears wiggle. "Astonishing," he said. "All these years on this moon, and not once did we ever encounter a live one. It's as if this particular one were waiting for us to . . ."

A rumbling sound echoed throughout the vast underground chamber. Before Nuru could order one of the troopers to bring Veeren back to the *Harpy*, the landing platform's surface buckled and exploded, and another whuffa's monstrous head rose up from the dust. A moment later, two other sections of platform near the *Harpy* shattered to reveal more whuffas. Veeren grabbed Nuru's arm as she cried, "They're everywhere!"

More whuffas appeared. The three troopers and Cleaver did not wait for Nuru to issue a command. They opened fire on the monsters, aiming for their mouths. Mcgrrrr whipped out his own blaster pistol and joined in the fight.

The whuffas had cut off any direct path back to the *Harpy*. Gazing past the whuffas, Nuru saw Gunn and Chatterbox in the *Harpy*'s cockpit. He waved his arm to get Chatterbox's attention, then made a series of quick gestures with his hand, signaling Chatterbox to launch the *Harpy* away from the spherical station.

The *Harpy*'s thrusters roared. The transport practically leaped as it left the landing pad and flew in reverse to exit the station. The pirate ships and the Sullustans' saucer saw the departing transport and were quick to follow its lead.

As Breaker, Sharp, Knuckles, Cleaver, and

Mcgrrrr continued firing at the incoming whuffas, Nuru looked at Groob and shouted, "Take us to the controls! Now!"

Groob scurried for the triangular doorway and into the corridor that he had pointed out earlier. Nuru and Veeren ran after him. Mcgrrrr and the troopers followed, with Cleaver at the rear, providing protective fire. The droid walked backward into the corridor so he could keep his photoreceptors and rifle trained on the whuffas.

A whuffa rammed its head into the doorway's triangular frame. Cleaver continued walking backward as he emptied his blaster rifle's energy charge into the monster's head. The whuffa released a rush of foul air into the corridor as it exhaled its last breath.

Groob, Nuru, and Veeren were the first to arrive at the chamber that contained the station's controls. Set on the angled surface of a stone pedestal, the controls included a set of green crystals and gold metal levers that were positioned next to two illuminated green indents. Each indent was an impression from the right hand of a three-fingered, clawed creature. A large, stone-framed viewscreen, which vaguely resembled a half-open eye, was built into the wall beside the pedestal.

As the three troopers, Mcgrrrr, and Cleaver arrived at the end of the corridor, Groob motioned for Nuru to join him behind the controls. Groob said, "Place your hand here!" He pointed to the first green indent.

"But that's the impression of a large lizard's claw," Nuru protested. "It was designed for the Kwa, not for—"

Nuru was interrupted by a loud thud from behind a nearby wall. Realizing that the whuffas might soon be upon them, Groob said, "No time to argue!" He grabbed Nuru's right wrist and shoved the Jedi's hand down into the first indent.

A humming sound came from within the pedestal, and then its crystals glowed brightly. Nuru felt a strange warmth travel up the length of his arm. The eye-shaped viewscreen blinked on, and a galactic star chart came into focus.

"It works!" Groob said. "Now, if you adjust this lever, you should be able to plot a course away from here. Then place your right hand in *this* indent to open the Infinity Gate."

Nuru pushed at one lever, and the star chart on the viewscreen appeared to rotate. As all eyes turned to the viewscreen, the star chart slid away, and was replaced by a view of a single solar system.

Mcgrrrr asked, "Anyone recognize that system?"

Before anyone could respond, a louder thud came from overhead, and a crack formed across the control chamber's ceiling. Veeren looked at Nuru and said, "Hurry. Just do what you must to get us out of here."

Without any idea of the consequences, Nuru moved his right hand into the second indent.

A thunderous crack sounded from beyond the corridor. Groob said, "It's done. The Infinity Gate is open. We have to get back to our ships."

Leaving the controls, Nuru led the group back into the corridor. He said, "Breaker, contact Chatterbox. Tell him to pick us up at the edge of the landing pad."

As Breaker used his helmet's comlink to summon Chatterbox, Cleaver walked up beside Nuru and said, "Commander, I regret to inform you that I left a dead whuffa blocking the doorway at the end of this corridor. How will we get out?"

Without breaking his stride, Nuru looked ahead and replied, "It appears the other whuffa have already taken care of that problem for us."

Cleaver and the others saw the doorway was clear. Marks on the floor indicated the corpse had been dragged away. Nuru said, "I don't know how smart the whuffas are, but I suspect they know this is the only exit."

Cleaver said, "Commander, I further regret that I depleted my weapon's power supply."

"Perhaps this might be useful," Nuru said. He reached to his belt, removed Ring-Sol Ambase's lightsaber, and handed it to the droid. "Cleaver, do what you can to create a diversion."

"Yes, sir," Cleaver said. Carrying the lightsaber, he stepped through the doorway.

The dead whuffa had not been hauled far from the corridor's entrance, and lay just a short distance away from Cleaver. The droid automatically counted seventeen live whuffas waiting on the landing platform, their horrific heads poised facing the doorway. He calculated the respective distance between their positions, then activated the lightsaber and sprinted for the nearest whuffa. As he leaped past the monster, he swung the lightsaber through two of the whuffa's thick teeth. The whuffa howled. In an instant, all the whuffas were surging across the platform, chasing after Cleaver.

Nuru motioned for Veeren, Mcgrrrr, Groob, and the three troopers to stop in the corridor behind him as he peered out from the doorway. He made sure Cleaver had effectively lured the whuffas to the far side of the landing platform, then looked to the platform's edge. Beyond the platform, shimmering lights danced in the air of the vast underground chamber. The lights reminded him of . . .

Hyperspace!

Nuru didn't know how long the Infinity Gate would remain open. *Where's the Harpy?* he wondered.

Breaker moved up beside Nuru just in time to see Gunn's transport descend to a low hover. The *Harpy*'s ramp was already extended. Breaker said, "There's our ride."

"Let's go," Nuru said. He grabbed Vereen's arm, pulling her along with him as he bolted for the hovering transport. Groob and Mcgrrrr went next, followed by the troopers. Breaker cast a quick glance in Cleaver's direction as he ran behind Sharp and Knuckles.

Chatterbox stood waiting at the top of the *Harpy*'s ramp. Nuru helped Veeren onto the ramp, then made sure Mcgrrrr and Groob got on, too. Chatterbox guided the passengers through the open hatch until Nuru came to a stop beside him. Nuru and Chatterbox watched Knuckles, Sharp, and Breaker approach, but then Breaker stopped and said, "Cleaver."

Nuru followed Breaker's gaze to see Cleaver swinging Ambase's lightsaber at the whuffas. Two whuffas lunged at Cleaver, but the droid leaped up into the air and the whuffas collided with each other instead. Cleaver twisted his body in midair, landed on a whuffa's back, and bounced off, angling toward the waiting *Harpy*. He switched off the lightsaber and hit the ground running.

As the whuffas charged after the fleeing droid, Knuckles and Sharp scampered up onto the ramp. They moved past Nuru and Chatterbox, who remained braced outside the transport. Facing Breaker, Nuru said, "Come on."

"I'm waiting for Cleaver."

"Move, Breaker. That's an order."

Breaker scrambled onto the ramp. The *Harpy* began to pull away from the landing platform. Seeing Cleaver running toward the platform's edge, Breaker shouted, "Jump!"

A whuffa was actually gaining on Cleaver as the droid leaped from the platform's edge, his arms extended in front of him. His outstretched metal fingers missed the *Harpy*'s platform and he began to fall.

Seeing the droid plummet, Breaker shouted, "No!"

But just then Cleaver appeared to bounce off an invisible cushion of air, and he soared up toward Breaker. Breaker did not pause to wonder how Cleaver had become airborne, but held tight to the side of the *Harpy* with one hand as he caught the droid's left wrist with the other, then he swung Cleaver up onto the ramp beside him. Only then did Breaker notice Nuru—still braced beside Chatterbox—had his right hand directed toward Cleaver. Breaker realized Nuru had used the Force to catch Cleaver and yank him back to the ship.

Cleaver followed Breaker's gaze and said, "Thank you, Commander Nuru."

"Thank me later!" Nuru said as he and Chatterbox hauled Breaker and Cleaver into the *Harpy*. The ramp lifted and the hatch sealed. Nuru ran through the main cabin, passing Groob, Knuckles, and Sharp, and didn't stop running until he'd reached the cockpit. Gunn and Mcgrrrr were seated behind the controls, and Veeren stood behind Gunn's seat.

Nuru looked through the cockpit window and saw the pirate ships in front of them, hovering near the side of the immense, glowing sphere as lights continued to shimmer throughout the chamber. Then the lights swirled and converged into a vortex. Veeren gasped at the sight.

"It's a hyperspace portal," Nuru said. "Mcgrrrr, hail the other ships. Tell them to fly into the portal."

"But where will we go?"

"With any luck, far from here," Gunn said. "Just do it!"

Mcgrrrr hailed the other ships. The pathfinders moved forward, then vanished into the vortex, followed by the Sullustans' saucer, the pirate starfighters, and the *Random Mallet*.

"Here goes nothing," Gunn said as she sent her transport into the vortex.

The *Harpy* shuddered as it plunged into a brilliant cascade of energy, and then a loud, harmonic whine traveled through the ship. Mcgrrrr said, "What was that noise?"

"Beats me," Gunn said as she checked her consoles. "I've never heard it before."

Listening carefully, Nuru said, "That noise isn't coming from the ship. It's from . . . outside."

"Sure doesn't sound like hyperspace to me," Gunn said. "I wonder how long it's gonna—"

Before Gunn could finish, the noise faded out, the cascade of light vanished, and the *Harpy* emerged into outer space, surrounded by stars. Through the cockpit window, the pirate vessels and the Sullustans' saucer were all in view.

Gunn said, "Where's the nebula and the black hole? That jump barely lasted thirty seconds. We couldn't have jumped far." She glanced at her scopes, then added, "My compass must still be on the blink. The readout says we're back in Chiss space."

Mcgrrrr said, "Then . . . we're free from the black hole!"

Nuru sensed Veeren become tense beside him. Her red eyes were locked on something outside the ship, beyond the pirate vessels. And then Nuru saw what she saw, too.

A large silhouette of an inverted conical station was suspended against the stars.

"There's nothing wrong with the compass, Gunn," Nuru said. "See over there? We've arrived back at the Chiss space station."

Mcgrrrr looked at Gunn and said, "Chiss space? And where exactly is that in relation to . . . anywhere?"

Ignoring Mcgrrrr, Gunn muttered, "It's not possible." Turning to Nuru, she repeated, "It's not possible! It took us almost ten hours to travel from Chiss space to the black hole sector." She shook her head. "How could we have covered that distance again so much faster?"

"We didn't use an Infinity Gate the first time," Nuru replied.

Mcgrrrr looked at a console. "No readings from that space station," he said, "but we are picking up a signal from a ship beside it. A Metalorn yacht."

Nuru said, "That's Umbrag's ship." Closing his eyes, he reached out with the Force, searching for any psychic trace of Ring-Sol Ambase. He sensed no sign of his missing Master.

"But where's the rest of Umbrag's fleet?" Gunn said. "There's no sign of them."

Mcgrrrr asked, "Who's Umbrag?"

"Bad guy," Gunn said. "We don't like him."

Mcgrrrr grinned. "Then my pirates and I don't like him, either."

The Skakoan Overseer Umbrag was sitting on the bridge of his Metalorn yacht, polishing his metal-rimmed goggles, when a skeletal battle droid stepped up to him and said, "Five starships and seven starfighters are heading this way, sir. The largest ship is a frigate."

"I wasn't expecting any reinforcements," Umbrag said through his breathing apparatus.

"They aren't Separatist vessels, sir."

Umbrag's eyes went wide behind his goggles.

"Republic warships?"

"Negative, sir. I think they're pirates."

Before Umbrag could respond, a large explosion wracked his entire yacht, launching him out of his seat. Umbrag grunted as he crashed to the floor.

The droid said, "That sounded like a concussion missile!"

Rising to his feet, Umbrag shoved the droid aside and stepped toward a console that displayed a stream of data beside twelve blips that represented the incoming ships. "Count Dooku told me that no one would approach this station after I claimed it!" Umbrag fumed. "I wouldn't have followed Dooku's orders and sent my armada back to Skako if I'd known there was any possibility of an attack!"

Another explosion rocked the yacht. The droid cried, "Perhaps Count Dooku was mistaken, sir?"

Umbrag launched his armored fist into the droid's head. As the droid stumbled away from him, Umbrag turned to face two more droids who stood before the navigation controls and shouted, "Get us out of here! Back to Skako! Now!"

The yacht's engines fired, then it sped away from the Chiss space station. The yacht took three more violent hits before it vanished into hyperspace.

The remaining ships circled the area of the yacht's departure, then turned and angled back, heading for the conical space station. They were still moving toward the station when sixty Chiss assault cruisers dropped out of hyperspace to surround them from all sides.

CHAPTER 11

"You and all your companions are free to leave," Veeren said.

She was standing in a large docking bay on the Chiss space station, facing Nuru, Captain Mcgrrrr, and Professor Groob. The *Hasty Harpy* rested on a platform near Nuru's group, and the Sullustans' saucer and a shuttle from the *Random Mallet* were parked on neighboring platforms. Breaker, Sharp, and Cleaver stood at the bottom of the *Harpy*'s ramp, watching Nuru and waiting for his return.

Mcgrrrr lifted his eyebrows and said, "You mean, you're letting the Black Hole Pirates loose?"

"Correct," Veeren said. "Although the Chiss

Ascendancy acknowledges that none of you were responsible for the Separatist attack, and also appreciates your combined effort to return me to Chiss space, make no mistake in the fact that none of you are entirely welcome here."

Mcgrrrr said, "I suppose that means you wouldn't be happy if I left Bossk behind?"

"I most certainly would not," Veeren answered coolly.

"I was jesting!" Mcgrrrr said with a chuckle. "I have every intention of releasing him from his commission as soon as we return to Republic space. But tell me, how are my pirates supposed to leave when I don't even know where Chiss space *is*?"

"Your respective navigators have received hyperspace coordinates that will deliver you to the edge of Republic space. From there, you may rely on the data in your own navi-computers."

Groob said, "Well, *I'm* certainly eager to get going. My family and I want very much to return to Sullust." He bowed politely to Veeren, then trotted off to his saucer.

Mcgrrrr turned to Nuru and said, "How do I know you won't come chasing after us?"

"I have no quarrel with you, Mcgrrrr," Nuru replied. "Bossk, on the other hand . . ."

Mcgrrrr laughed and clapped Nuru on the shoulder. "I wish you only clear skies, lad, but if the Jedi business doesn't work out for you, I hope you'll let me know." Then he leaned closer to Nuru and added, "In my humble opinion, you would make an excellent pirate."

Mcgrrrr walked off to his shuttle. Nuru looked at Veeren. He had so many things he wanted to ask her, but remembering his responsibilities as a Jedi, he chose his words carefully. "Good-bye, Aristocra. I regret that my mission to Chiss space did not go at all well, but I am relieved that the Separatists did not destroy your station, and that no Chiss lives were lost in the attack. I shall inform my superiors that Republic ships should stay out of Chiss space until you decide to renew diplomatic discussions."

Just then, the Sullustans' saucer and Mcgrrrr's shuttle rose up from the landing platform, and traveled out through the docking bay's shielded portal and into space. Nuru glanced at the departing ships, then returned his attention to Veeren.

"Good-bye, Nuru Kungurama."

Once again, Nuru noticed Veeren's upper lip sneered slightly as she said his name. He said, "Wait, Aristocra. Forgive me for asking, but I am curious . . . Does my name irritate you in some way?"

Veeren stared hard at Nuru for a moment, then replied, "The Jedi did not read the data cylinder correctly."

Confused, Nuru said, "I don't understand."

"You told me that a Jedi found you in a Chiss escape pod when you were an infant, and that the Jedi learned your name from a data cylinder. But your name is not Nuru Kungurama. You are Kung'urama'nuruodo of the Second Ruling Family."

"Oh," Nuru said. "Oh! And . . . You are of the Second Ruling Family, too, and your name also ends with *nuruodo*. Does that mean we're . . . related?"

Veeren arched one eyebrow. "That is a tactless question," she said.

Nuru did not know how to respond, but knowing that he might never see Veeren again he felt compelled to say something. "I'm sorry I don't know Chiss protocol," he said. "I wish we could have talked more. I realize you may not care to hear this, but . . . I am glad we met."

"I know," Veeren said. And then she turned and walked away, heading for a door on the other side of the docking bay. The door slid open, and she stepped through it without looking back.

Nuru walked back to the *Harpy*. Seeing his approach, Breaker, Sharp, and Cleaver stepped away from the transport's ramp. Cleaver held Ring-Sol Ambase's lightsaber out to Nuru and said, "I neglected to return this to you earlier, Commander."

"Thank you, Cleaver," Nuru said as he took the weapon and clipped it to his belt beside his own lightsaber. "And I neglected to tell you that you handled yourself very well against the whuffa."

"Thank you, sir," Cleaver said. The droid and Breaker turned and walked up the ramp.

Nuru was about to follow when Sharp said, "One moment, Commander." He removed his helmet and stepped closer to Nuru.

Nuru could see from his knitted brow that he was very concerned. "What's wrong, Sharp?"

"I've been thinking about how we arrived at that black hole, sir," Sharp said, keeping his voice low. "I hate to say this, but I can't stop wondering if either Chatterbox or Captain Gunn had something to do with it. Maybe one of them rigged the navi-computer. Maybe both of them rigged it."

Astonished, Nuru said, "But . . . why?"

"I don't know, sir," Sharp said. "But I don't think we wound up near that black hole by accident, and I believe they were the only ones who could have done the job to get us there."

Nuru shook his head. "I don't know what to say, Sharp. The facts don't add up. I mean, *why* would Gunn or Chatterbox do it? Also, they were both on the *Harpy* while we were in the Star Chamber's control station. They had nothing to do with adjusting the controls to the Infinity Gate that delivered us back here. *I* did that, though I don't know exactly how. I suppose it was an incredibly fortunate accident."

"But think about it, Commander," Sharp said. "Doesn't it seem overly coincidental that we would *accidentally* arrive near the black hole, only to encounter people who would lead you to a Star Chamber so you could *accidentally* deliver us straight back to Chiss space?"

Nuru's eyes went wide. "You think we're being manipulated?"

"I do, sir," Sharp said. "And I'd like very much to know who's pulling the strings. Meanwhile, I suggest we watch both Chatterbox and Gunn very carefully."

"Perhaps we should confide with Breaker and Cleaver about this."

Sharp grimaced. "Now that I think of it, Breaker's awfully keen with technology. What if he's the saboteur?"

Nuru had a hard time thinking of Breaker as a suspect. "We . . . we shouldn't jump to conclusions." He gestured to the landing ramp. "Come on. We'd better get aboard before the others start suspecting that *we're* up to something."

Sharp followed Nuru onto the *Harpy*. The ship lifted off to exit the docking bay, then traveled to the designated hyperspace portal. As Gunn's transport launched into hyperspace, Nuru contemplated Sharp's concerns. And the more he thought about it, the more he began to suspect that someone was indeed manipulating the actions of the Breakout Squad.

But who?

"Nuru Kungurama and Breakout Squad successfully returned the Aristocra to Chiss space," Count Dooku said. "And with the aid of the Sullustan xenoarchaelologist and Mcgrrrr's gang, they forced Overseer Umbrag to retreat."

Dooku was standing in his secret lair, facing the flickering hologram of Darth Sidious that was suspended in the air before him. A dark hood concealed the upper half of Darth Sidious's face, but Dooku could clearly see his Master's lips twitch into a sick smile.

"Those ridiculous pirates and their allies served us well," Darth Sidious said. "They believed themselves cursed by the forces of a black hole that held them captive in space, never realizing that their arrival in that remote sector was *not* an accident . . . never knowing the truth. It was *we* who cursed them."

His smile vanished. "Everything is proceeding as I have foreseen," he continued. "All of our pawns—including Nuru Kungurama—have unknowingly served us well in the years that have led up to this moment. It is only a matter of time before we form an alliance with the Chiss."

Facing the hologram, Dooku hesitated for a moment, then said, "The Trandoshan hunter's arrival near the black hole nearly disrupted our plan."

"His arrival was necessary," Darth Sidious snapped. "It was our best opportunity to introduce him to Kungurama."

Lifting his eyebrows, Dooku said, "And now that they've met?"

"They must meet again," Darth Sidious replied softly. "It is only . . . natural." Then the Sith Lord leered and added, "And speaking of reunions, how is your guest?"

"He's coming around."

"Excellent. Keep me apprised."

"Yes, my Master," Dooku said just before Darth Sidious's hologram vanished.

CHAPTER 12

Ring-Sol Ambase opened his eyes slowly. He felt groggy, and his throat was very dry.

He was lying on his back on an elevated pad in a dimly illuminated room with a white, octagonal ceiling. He tried to lift and turn his head, but felt a pressure against the lower half of his face. Something covered his nose and mouth.

A breath mask?

He blinked and wondered where he was. And then his mind flooded with his last memory before he had lost consciousness.

Nuru!

He had no idea how his young Padawan

apprentice had wound up on board the unarmed freighter that had transported him and three squads of clone troopers to the planet Kynachi. During the transit through hyperspace, he had sensed Nuru's presence, and even informed a clone trooper named Breaker about the nagging sensation, but Breaker had assured him that no other Jedi was on the ship.

And then the freighter had arrived at Kynachi, only to be attacked by a waiting armada of Separatist warships. A few troopers were killed immediately. Ambase recalled ordering the surviving clones to go to the escape pods, and how surprised he had been—just before his own pod had jettisoned—to sense Nuru again, using the Force to call out to him. But then Ambase's pod had fallen away from the shattered freighter, and beyond that, his memory was blank.

Ambase was certain that his Padawan had been on the freighter. But he had no idea whether Nuru had survived.

Where am I?

He shifted his gaze from the ceiling. He was lying on a conform pad, covered by a white blanket. Medical diagnostic machines with winking lights were on either side of him. From what he could see, he was lying in the center of an eight-walled room with a single window that offered a view of a gray sky. He was unable to see any doors, but suspected one might be set into the wall behind the head of his conform pad.

He studied the diagnostic machines again, trying to comprehend their functions. *What happened? How long have I been here?*

He tried to move his arms and legs. The blanket did not shift even slightly over his inert body, which seemed dead below his neck. One of the machines began beeping, and he wondered if his attempt to move had triggered an alarm of some kind. And then he became aware of a presence.

Someone had entered the room. The beeping noise continued. Ambase tried to speak, but his throat felt dry and weak.

"Please remain still, Master Ambase," a deep voice said from the unseen area behind him. "You've been through a great deal."

Ambase recognized the voice instantly. He saw a tall figure move into view to the left of his bed. His eyes went wide as he directed his gaze to the man who had once been not only a Jedi Master, but also his friend.

Dooku.

"Ring-Sol, *please*," Dooku said in an imploring tone. "I sense your anxiety, but I beg you to not move."

Because Ambase had already realized that he was immobilized, he found Dooku's plea almost amusing.

"Your pulmonary system has been damaged," Dooku continued. "I assure you that I am not responsible for your present condition, and that you are not my prisoner. I will even arrange for your immediate and safe return to the Jedi Temple, if that is what you desire. All I ask is that you allow me to explain how you arrived at my retreat."

Dooku's retreat? Ambase did not trust Dooku, but also knew he was at the man's mercy. Keeping his eyes fixed on the renegade Jedi, he took a deep, calming breath, and then another. A moment later, the nearby machine stopped beeping, indicating that Ambase's pulmonary system had stabilized.

Dooku offered a sympathetic smile. "I know you don't trust me, Ring-Sol. You believe I was wrong to leave the Jedi Order. You told me so yourself at the time." Dooku's smile melted away as his brow furrowed. "You also believe that I'm responsible for the battle on Geonosis, and for all the terrible things that have happened since. I have no illusions that you think me a turncoat and murderer."

Ambase thought, *You can't imagine what I think of you.*

Looking away from Ambase, Dooku stared at the window. "I won't waste your time with further explanations for my reasons for leaving the Jedi Order, or try to convince you that it was not I who started this terrible war." Returning his gaze to Ambase, Dooku added, "If I could go back in time and change things, I would."

Dooku stepped over to the window, his elegant cape shifting behind him as he moved. Looking back at Ambase, he said, "On Geonosis, I informed Obi-Wan Kenobi that hundreds of Senators have fallen under the influence of a Sith Lord called Darth Sidious, and that the Republic is under the control of the Sith. I had evidence that Darth Sidious was in league with the Viceroy of the Trade Federation, but betrayed him. I tried to warn the Jedi Council, but they wouldn't listen to me. I sought Kenobi's help to destroy the Sith, but he refused. I wonder . . . Did the Jedi Council inform you about this?"

Ambase remained silent.

"Forgive me," Dooku said. "I forgot, your voice has not yet returned. I don't mean to put any strain on you, Ring-Sol, but perhaps you could blink your eyes to respond? One blink for yes, and two blinks for no?"

Ambase willed himself to keep his eyes open.

"Were you told about Darth Sidious?"

Unwilling to yield any information, Ambase continued staring at Dooku.

Dooku frowned. "As I told Obi-Wan on Geonosis, the dark side of the Force has clouded the Council's vision. It wouldn't surprise me if they chose to remain silent about Darth Sidious."

Moving away from the window, Dooku returned to Ambase's bedside. "It was never my wish to fight the Jedi, Ring-Sol. Nor did I aspire to divide the Republic, or lead the Separatists. But in the end, if we don't choose our battles, the battles choose us. Ever since I learned of Darth Sidious, my goal has remained nothing less than to stop the Sith from conquering the galaxy. I can't do it alone."

Ambase was unable to detect whether Dooku

was lying. All he could do was keep listening.

"I'm telling you all this," Dooku continued, "because I suspect you, too, may have been betrayed, possibly by someone close to you. But I don't expect you to take my word for it. You should listen to the individual who brought you here."

Dooku nodded in the direction of the wall that Ambase could not see. Ambase heard footsteps approach, and a moment later four BX-series droid commandos escorted a dark-haired man into the chamber. From where he lay, Ambase saw that the man wore a gray tunic and that his face was that of a clone from Kamino.

Ambase could barely believe his eyes. *A clone? Is he allied with Dooku?*

"General Ambase," the clone said softly, "are you all right?"

Ambase only glared in return. The clone seemed to see the alarm in the Jedi Master's eyes, and added, "I . . . I'm afraid I can't remember exactly how we got here, sir."

Dooku said, "I imagine you two have much to discuss. The droids and I shall wait outside." Dooku's cape flowed behind him as he led the droid commandos from the chamber.

Facing Ambase and keeping his voice low, the clone said, "General Ambase, I . . . I realize Dooku may have recording devices in this room, but . . . you need to know what's happened. Maybe you remember the explosions after our freighter arrived in Kynachi's orbit, how we went to the escape pods. Well, someone must have rigged the pods so they wouldn't eject, at least not immediately. The ones that managed to get away filled up with some kind of knockout gas. By the time I got a breath mask on you, you were already unconscious."

The clone glanced at the doorway, then continued, "Our pod made it to Kynachi, but we were captured by droids. They took you away from us and threw us in prison.

Ambase listented intently but felt himself fighting to stay awake.

"Fortunately," the clone continued, "a few troopers had evaded the droids, and they came to get us. A young Jedi was with them, identified himself as Nuru Kungurama. Said he was your apprentice. I didn't know how he arrived on Kynachi—not at the time, that is—but we were all relieved to see a Jedi. The Republic troops liberated Kynachi, sir. We tried to find you, but then . . . I'm afraid something bad must have happened."

Ambase watched the clone grimace. He did not require the Force to see the man was deeply troubled.

"I remember searching for you, and then I must have blacked out." The clone shook his head, as if the motion might jog a memory. "When I came to, I had a nasty bump on the back of my head, and I was in the cockpit of a crashed Kuat transport. I have no memory at all of flying it, but I was seated behind the controls. I found you unconscious, strapped down to a bunk in the hold. The comm system was shattered. Distress beacons had already been launched. Unfortunately, the distress beacons brought droid commandos, who captured me. But before they arrived, I also found this."

The clone reached to his belt and removed a small cylinder. "It's the freighter's log, sir, the freighter that was destroyed at Kynachi. The log contains holorecordings. The droids took the log from me, along with my armor and weapons. I tried to fight them, but there were just too many. They must have handed the log over to Dooku because the next thing I knew, he showed up in my cell, asking me to explain what happened on the final holorecording. I think you should see it, sir."

Holding the cylinder with one hand, the clone thumbed a switch and the cylinder's top slid back to project a hologram in the air above Ambase's outstretched form. The clone then adjusted the angle of the cylinder so Ambase could see the hologram clearly.

Dark metal walls, blinking lights . . . Ambase recognized the three-dimensional image as a representation of a comm station in a narrow corridor on the freighter that had carried him and the doomed troopers to Kynachi.

A bright burst of light appeared, and a split second later, the small cylinder produced the recorded sound of an explosion. Ambase realized he was viewing the corridor at the moment the Separatists had opened fire on the freighter. He heard an unseen clone trooper cry out, and then there was another flash, followed by another explosive noise.

The recording showed a utility closet door flying open, and then the image of a young, robed boy tumbling out of the closet. The boy had blue skin and red eyes. Ambase recognized him instantly.

Nuru.

Although the clone at his bedside claimed Nuru had survived the explosion, Ambase watched in horror as the flickering image of his apprentice fell toward a holographic trooper. The trooper reached for Nuru and shouted, "Hang on!" Another bright light flashed, and then the hologram flickered out.

Ambase redirected his gaze at the clone who stood beside him.

"You saw where the boy was hiding, sir? That utility closet had access to the freighter's engineering station. Forgive me for asking, General, but . . . Do you think it's possible your apprentice might have sabotaged the freighter?"

Sabotage? Nuru?!

The clone noticed Ambase's mouth tremble under the breath mask. Ambase lifted his head slightly from the cushion as he stared hard at the trooper and gasped, "Whuh . . . What . . ."

A health monitor began beeping again, followed by Dooku's voice. "Ring-Sol?"

Ambase had not even heard Dooku's approach, but suddenly realized Dooku had already returned to his beside. Dooku said, "Perhaps we should leave you to rest."

Ignoring Dooku, Ambase struggled to remain focused on the trooper's face and finally managed to rasp out, "What is . . . your name?"

The trooper leaned closer to Ambase's face and said, "I'm sorry, General. I shouldn't have expected you to remember me. We were never introduced, but I was seated across from you in the freighter on the Kynachi mission. They call me Sharp."

Ambase winced, and then his eyes closed as his head fell back against the cushion.

Dooku glanced from Ambase to the trooper, then consulted one of the diagnostic monitors. The health monitor stopped beeping. "He's unconscious again," Dooku said, "but his condition remains stable. He *will* recover." Then Dooku looked at the clone and said, "I trust you're doing well under the circumstances?"

The clone replied, "Never better."

For Henry Gilroy.

Big thanks to Jason Fry, coauthor with Dan Wallace of Star Wars: The Essential Atlas *(Del Rey, 2009), who generously plotted the hyperspace routes used in this story.*

NEXT:

Star Wars: The Clone Wars
Secret Missions #3:
Duel at Shattered Rock

After the young Jedi Nuru Kungurama and the clone troopers of Breakout Squad leave Chiss space, they receive orders to escort new allies across space to Coruscant. But the diplomatic mission turns deadly when the identity of the mysterious saboteur is at last revealed, and Nuru encounters a deadly armored warrior with ties to Count Dooku.

ABOUT THE AUTHOR

A former editor of *Star Wars* and *Indiana Jones* comics, Ryder Windham has written more than sixty books, including *Star Wars: The Ultimate Visual Guide* (DK Publishing), *Star Wars: The Life and Legend of Obi-Wan Kenobi* (Scholastic), and *Indiana Jones and the Pyramid of the Sorcerer* (Harper Collins UK and Scholastic). He lives in Providence, Rhode Island, with his family.

ABOUT THE COVER ARTIST

Wayne Lo served as Art Director on the video game *Lair* as well as spent six years in Industrial Light & Magic's art department, where he cursed pirates, skinned werewolves, skewered vampires, and thawed Neverland, before joining the design team for Lucasfilm's *Star Wars: The Clone Wars* animated series.